Previous Praise for Colin

The Thirteenth Month is a su[...]
travelogue, bibliography, and kunstlerroman, it contains the research
and lore of a great essay, the depth of a metaphysical poem, but the
soul of a novel ... Intelligent without pretension, worldly without
condescension, Hamilton renders both scenes and mindscapes with
equal mastery of the terrain.

Phong Nguyen, author of *Pages from the Textbook of Alternative History* and *The Adventures of Joe Harper*

Colin Hamilton has combined the visible and the invisible into a truly
unusual first book ... The writing is exquisite, the mysteries engaging,
and the result original.

Marvin Bell, author of *The Book of the Dead Man* and *Nightworks: Poems 1962 — 2000*

The Thirteenth Month is a multiverse of mirrors and infinite texts
spanning the inevitable labyrinth that exists between a young man's
books and his reality. It belongs in the company of Borges, Pessoa,
and Schulz, the very writers Hamilton admires, all the while cleverly
disguised as an Iowan's bildungsroman.

Elizabeth McKenzie, author of *The Portable Veblen*

This is a sophisticated hybrid of Borgesian imagination and heartbroken, yet dry-eyed, memoir ... 'touched by the divine finger of poetry' himself, [Hamilton] writes with admirable grace, clarity, and appetite, whether about invisible cities or his mother's fighting dementia.

DeWitt Henry, *Ploughshares*

Masterfully conceived and effortlessly rendered, Colin Hamilton has given us a delightfully enthralling and immersive account of the power of narrative to elucidate and transform the world. I relished every page.

Matthew Vollmer, author of *Future Missionaries of America* and *Permanent Exhibit*

The poetry, page after page, is of the kind that keeps the reader on the critical edge, both ecstatic and lucid, both active and illumined ... Nothing more exotic here than the beauty of utterance set free.

Stavros Deligiorgis

The Discarded

The Discarded

Colin Hamilton

UNBOUND EDITION PRESS

Atlanta

Copyright © 2024 by Colin Hamilton
All Rights Reserved

FIRST EDITION

Printed in the United States of America

LIBRARY OF CONGRESS RECORD

Name: Hamilton, Colin, 1969 — author.
Title: The Discarded / Colin Hamilton.
Edition: First edition.
Published: Atlanta : Unbound Edition Press, 2024.

LCCN: 2023935043
LCCN Permalink: https://lccn.loc.gov/2023935043
ISBN: 979-8-9870199-3-1 (fine softcover)

Designed by Eleanor Safe and Joseph Floresca
Printed by Bookmobile, Minneapolis, MN
Distributed by Itasca Books

23456789

Unbound Edition Press
1270 Caroline Street, Suite D120
Box 448
Atlanta, GA 30307

*The Unbound Edition Press logo and name are
registered trademarks of Unbound Edition LLC.*

For Helena

A cicada shell;
it sang itself
utterly away.

MATSUO BASHŌ
trans. Robert Hass

Contents

A Library Within Our Library	19
Under the Raven by Josef Matousek	29
Coiling and Recoiling: An Anthology of Anthro-Reptilian Eroticism by Shikha Sen	41
The Threaded Trail by Amalia Delicari	51
Six-Legged Stars by Sylvia Armentrout	59
This Is Not a Biography: The Life of David Markson by Jasper De Jong	69
Tortured by Roses by M. K. Suzuki	85
Killing Time by Cesar Alvarez	97
Further Adventures in the Unknown Interior by Javier Sandoval	107
Where Angels Reign: A Record of My Voyage through the Southern Seas with the Purported Scientist Charles Darwin by Hammish Mountolive	125

A Mind of Winter by Antonia Wallace	137
An Interruption	145
Fodder by Komas Dalaho	155
The Frivolous Ones by Ichiro Takamine	165
A Guide to Universal Grasping by Nathan Park	177
The Hell of Insects by Michael Maroun	185
Leopold's Jungle by Mats Vandroogenbroeck	193
The Lucky One by Hyacinthe Danse	203
Days of 1931 by Vasilis Vasilakis	219
A Museum of Winter	231
The Great Balzoni Disappears by Aron Schmitz	237
A History of Book Burning by Lynn Pearson	253

The
Discarded

A Library Within Our Library

At the turn of this millennium's second decade, our central library was a tired, yellowish building, all linoleum and worn brass. Its wiring had become so frayed it could only sustain the dimmest of bulbs, and as patrons wandered back into the remote stacks, where the old books with their faded spines rested undisturbed, they drifted into darker and darker recesses. Neither our prized collection nor the drift of patrons through the aisles, neither the old men made a little mad by the cold and loneliness who warmed themselves in the atrium nor the young woman whose lips moved ever so slightly while she read the opening chapters of *My Brilliant Friend* could awaken it.

The library had fallen into this exhausted state some time before. Actually, it had been declared a disappointment by virtually everyone almost as soon as it had opened, but given its base functionality and ability to avoid prolonged attention, to disappoint without stirring action, and given the hard reality that any true correction would require a formidable public investment, we learned to live with our disappointment. For some, a bad marriage is better than raising the kids alone.

But not for all. Periodically a proposal to tear the library down and begin anew would become the rallying cry of a visionary few, and then almost as quickly, as the markets would contract and tax dollars tighten, their energy would dissipate. When its finances finally resettled, the city would turn its attention to more urgent concerns like the construction of a new sports arena or the contested path of a planned light rail line.

Most of us, and especially those more prone to northern gloom, or those who managed our northern gloom through a practice of reassuring, preemptive pessimism, were in fact quite surprised when one summer everything that could be removed from the library was packed into crates and onto trolleys and loaded on trucks. The core of the historic collection was taken to an industrial storage facility, while the rest was moved just down the street into the middle floors of an underutilized office building where these items were, to the extent possible, reassembled into something library-like, albeit in a corporatized form, which would need to suffice until a new library could be built.

Meanwhile, bulldozers and a crane swinging a concrete ball the size of a great blue whale's skull — but much, much harder — reduced the building itself to rubble. The press reported that seventy-eight percent of the debris would be reclaimed and repurposed into low-rent housing or shipping containers, and for a brief moment our papers were filled with nostalgic letters to the editor about the building that, like old Aunt Leone, no one had loved until gone.

✢ ✢ ✢

Offered the chance to begin anew, our citizens expressed that the poor quality of our last library may have captured the pioneer frugality in which our history was rooted, but it had failed to equal our emerging sense of self as an oasis of culture and decency, not so much a colder Omaha but a misplaced Seattle, a future San Francisco. A cosmopolitan Argentine architect was hired to realize our dreams, which were voiced through varied listening sessions and community forums, on Post-it notes and whiteboards. And what did we want? Countless books on every topic imaginable, an abundant collection of computers, welcoming fireplaces. Comfortable chairs and natural light and kindness. A place where infants and toddlers could nestle in their parents' laps while rhyming words multiplied their nascent neural receptors, and somewhere else for teens to gather and play non-violent video games away from the lure of corrupting temptation. Easy access to the bus lines. An attached parking ramp would be nice too.

After three years of planning, revision, and construction, a new library rose up on the site of the demolished building. It was composed of two rectangles wedged at an angle so that at one end they nearly touched and at the other they opened into a grand, tilted face. The atrium created between these two wings, which soared five stories high, was capped by a white metal firmament that stretched from one city block to another, or actually a bit farther, tipping, on each side, beyond the building itself and over the adjacent streets. ("Won't snow come crashing down from the wing straight onto our cars?" people asked. "No," the architect assured us.) The facades were made of clear glass, etched on one side with the outlines of birch trees, on the others with wild prairie grasses, snow on boughs, and lake water. ("And what about the birds?" others inquired cautiously. "They are so lovely," he agreed.) Bands of yellow river stone ran lengthwise around the building, dividing its floors.

Inside, the layout of each floor mimicked the others with a broad central corridor lined by fourteen rows of computers that culminated in a grand fireplace, its glass case rising from floor to ceiling and surrounded by soft, welcoming chairs. A large information desk sat midway down each corridor. To both sides were aisles and aisles of books. Closer to the windows, the space gave way to small desks and workstations, the occasional study room. A few areas, the children's library, the teen center, and the athenaeum, had distinct characters all their own: playful and wild; cool and elevated; oaken.

✧ ✧ ✧

As a library aide, I spent the majority of my days working on varied research assignments and restocking the shelves, one of the few monotonous but unautomated tasks in this highly mechanized building. Picking up a cart of books from the returns room, I might on any given day bend to the right, passing under giant, suspended butterflies and ladybugs and into the forested children's library, or I might press forward into the glittering shelves of new arrivals, from which I'd eventually drift on to the realm of general fiction and its offshoots: romance, crime, fantasy. It was a garden of forking paths, and I could end anywhere from Soviet agricultural policy to the cargo cults of Melanesia.

On some occasions, however, rather than returning it to the collection, I would retrieve a cart from one of the division workrooms and wheel it to the service elevator and then ride that down to the second basement. Both subterranean floors were entirely devoid of the high design elements that brought the library itself into such vibrant existence. These hallways were just wide enough for whatever trolleys and equipment had been deemed necessary to pass through them, and from the dents and scrapes along the wall it was evident we'd either miscalculated or had hired people who hardly cared. The hallways remained dark and flickering despite the uncovered fluorescent bulbs that ran along the ceiling. The floors were bare, pockmarked concrete.

What drew me down into the basement lay at the end of a dark hall behind a final set of double doors. It was a large, nondescript room filled with rows of old metal shelving that had been scavenged from the prior library, everything gray and functional and pressed far closer together than any fire code would allow. When the new library first opened, this room was spotless and its shelves empty, but within months it began to fill, and within a year or so the shelves had become stacked haphazardly with books, thousands or possibly tens of thousands of books, some in horizontal piles, some slumped half vertically, some ready to tumble onto the floor, some already having tumbled onto the floor, all without order or design, simply massed. *Daylight. A Lady of Montevideo. Volcanic Islands of the Southern Pacific. Trade Secrets of Circus Engineering. Everything Nietzsche Left Unsaid. The World's Greatest Lies and Liars. Why and Why Not. A Week from Last Saturday. Never, Mr. Hobletzelle!*

The chaos of this room was disorienting, especially coming from the proper library, although it retained a particularly bookish variety of chaos — silent and undisturbed. What unified these books was that they had all been stripped from the library's permanent collection and were now waiting to be sold at quarterly sales for fifty cents or a dollar, sometimes in anonymous brown bags with their tops rolled down and stapled. Or shipped to Africa in vast containers. Or recycled for pulp.

Although rarely discussed publicly, an unavoidable reality of every library is that collections cannot simply grow and grow. Finite shelves fill and at some point the past begins to crowd out the possibility of new works and discoveries. As another architect once observed, the past is too small for the future to inhabit. Thus libraries weed, harvesting from their collection books that have been damaged or defaced, with missing pages or obscene drawings, with scribbled rhymes and insults crowding the margins; best sellers that had been bought en masse to satisfy one season's demand, but that were largely forgotten just a few years later, or easily reduced to a half dozen copies, or one; books of economic data, scientific reports, medical advice, political analysis that were no longer accurate or relevant.

Scattered among this refuse were also those books that had, for any number of reasons, despite holding a place on the shelves for years, occasionally even for decades, never managed to attract enough readers to justify their continued presence and in some cases, no readers whatsoever, perhaps not a single one. Although thousands of people — songwriters and nurses, immigrants and small business owners, poets and researchers, book clubbers and soloists, long-distance truck drivers, inventors, the brokenhearted, the aggrieved, the inexplicably hopeful, lawyers and job seekers, the curious, the introverts, those whose insomnia had kept them awake all night, those longing to escape into another dimension, those seeking a way back — passed through the library every day, they all, apparently, passed up the opportunity to read *The Least Coveted of Jewels*, *The Thorns of Reality*, or *A Lavish Pyre*.

And of course, most of the books were dreadful. Poorly designed, garish in their covers, outlandish in their blurbs, pedantic in their dust jacket summaries, awkward in their opening paragraphs, clumsy in their characters, clichéd in their final lines, stilted in their dialogue, ridiculous if not outright creepy in their sex. It is easy to understand why even those patrons who had deigned to handle them had — quickly, unceremoniously, with slight embarrassment — set them back down.

But sometimes there would be something else as well, a little glimmer of talent, of distinction, that might break through for a few pages before succumbing to the worst, or the most predictable, of writerly habits. And sometimes I really couldn't tell why one of these volumes had been banished while its peer had become a book club favorite. Many, despite their age, looked virtually new, with a clear, crisp stand to their spines, still glossy in their cellophane wraps, eagerly awaiting a reader.

One afternoon I started to pull a few of *these* books aside, four or five at first, and then a dozen or two. Not finding any open space, I created some, sweeping the top shelf of a far rack clear, and on it I began to assemble a second library scavenged out of all this waste. To begin, it was quite small, not even stretching from one vertical to the other, but each time I returned to the discard room, I'd excavate a few more discoveries and my library would expand incrementally, a few inches at a time, until it must have comprised a couple hundred books.

What were they? *The Metaphysics of Board Games, Volume 3: World Conquest. The Thirteenth Month. Disembodied Feet,* a critique of George Bush's post-presidential paintings by an Iraqi art historian.

Or more generally: idiosyncratic encyclopedias of obscure topics and histories; travel narratives that ended badly; grandiose lives that ended badly; social movements that ended badly; doubles and exchanged identities; old stories retold, creating the sense of a new possibility before collapsing back upon themselves; classical Greeks, medieval Britons, modernist Japanese, and futuristic Brazilians; science fiction imbued with the most conservative of values; thin books with fat themes; books by authors who produced only one, or who produced one that stood in general conflict with the rest of their oeuvre; books by authors who had written something magnificent in their first attempt and then helplessly repeated themselves through increasingly grotesque parodies; would-be scholarly volumes by authors rightfully marginalized in their fields; passion projects; detailed arguments that were not so much wrong as entirely ignorable.

There was a general disdain for realism, moderation, tact, and fact. Those had their own library above.

As I assembled this second library from the discards of the first, I tried to find some proper order for it, not dictated by Library of Congress call numbers but by some other, more personal sense of structure, by patterns and repetitions that ran through the books themselves. Just as I thought I was beginning to get that right, something curious happened: a few of the books disappeared, only to be returned a week or two later, near but not precisely where I had first positioned them. There wasn't much mystery to it. Although the discard room was nearly always empty when I returned to it, I knew that other librarians visited it as well on their breaks. In their meanderings, they must have come across these curated shelves and been drawn to them, maybe out of simple curiosity. And since it was also a library, they borrowed.

Very little happened at first, but before long, in the cafeteria room or up on the roof where we'd sometimes escape to smoke or sip coffees, I started to hear whispers about "the discard library" and "visiting the morgue." I had never really made anything before, and so I was flattered to hear the chatter, but I also felt a touch a sorrow, knowing that a moment was passing, as they do. Soon I noticed that my books weren't just disappearing from my shelves but that other books were being added as other librarians, also passing time down below, found among the refuse the odd title here or there they felt compelled to save.

Under the Raven
Josef Matousek (trans. Frederik Rosenkrantz)

From the very start, a favorite find was Josef Matousek's *Under the Raven*. It begins:

We are in a large, dark room, lit only by speckled columns of dusty, late-afternoon light filtering down through the cellar windows. There is the buzz of people speaking softly, slowly, possibly to themselves. Cigarette smoke snakes around the silhouetted men and women, pushing down the hoppy smell of beer as it rises up from the floor. It is not an office but a place where business of a certain kind can be done.

A man — we'll follow him — sits alone. It would be easy to say he's seen better days, but has he? He's seen many days, that's for sure, but how many were actually good or simply better than this? When he concentrates, he can feel his heart beating in his earlobes and fingertips, each surge of blood elbowing through the accumulated debris of drink and meat and tar. A single cough triggers a fit, and soon enough he's half doubled over, his fist and sleeve wet with whatever had recently clogged his lungs. Yes, there must have been better ones. He searches his brain for them, but all that comes back are clichés that belong to the collective memory rather than his actual past: fields of wheat in August, a wedding party, men singing with their arms around one another, children playing soccer.

When he rights himself, a woman has taken the seat across from him. Her hair is dyed black and stands stiff, her nose an inverted Slavic arch, her face pale and inviting. It's curious, he observes, that her lips haven't thinned with time and age. "Are you," she asks, "Vojacek?"

What he is is the type to indulge metaphysical questions, at least in the playground of his own mind, and so he immediately wonders, "Am I Vojacek? Or am I the one *called* Vojacek? What would it mean to *be* Vojacek? And just because I may have *been* Vojacek, what proof do I have that I *continue to be* Vojacek?" Although his job is to solve things, to get to the truth, what gives him the most pleasure these days are unanswerable inquiries.

Sensing, however, that the woman expects a more direct answer, he allows that he is.

"Good," she says with a visible sigh of relief. "I've been told you could help." He wonders if the casual way she twists a band of hair behind her ear would be more accurately described as "sensual" or "mechanical." It amuses him to be unsure, which leads to the subsequent thought: "Why should they be opposed?"

Returning to the moment, he acknowledges, "Perhaps. What seems to be amiss?"

She opens her mouth to speak, then pauses, then begins again only to be interrupted by an impatient waiter. She raises a finger to order, and he does the same after eyeing the foamy remnants in his glass. When she returns from this interlude, she has a hard time making eye contact, preferring now, it would seem, to stare into the table's gouged and gutted boards than this other's face.

"'What seems to be amiss?' Well, for some time now, several months or even half a year, I'm aware that I've simply felt less and less. Less pleasure for sure, but even ... anything. Anything at all. It's like the world is just a bit further away, out of reach;

I can observe things passing by me, but I no longer feel as though I am participating in its currents. I've all but stopped eating. And although I can perceive and even articulate some of these things, I have no ability to change them. I used to sometimes worry that I had no real purpose in this world, but it's gone deeper than that now. The word that keeps coming to mind is 'finished.'

"This may sound like a small thing, but I used to take a particular pleasure in recognizing faces as I went about my daily business, not so much people I knew, not friends or colleagues, but someone I'm certain I once dined beside, or made way for on a tram, or who rang me up at a counter. To find that person again, somewhere else, weeks or even months into the future — I could imagine how our two lives had, like unspooling threads, wound their way through this city and crossed at these unexpected, utterly trivial points. It meant nothing at all, but it assured me, in some small way, that my existence was wound into the fabric of this place; that everything I did, no matter how simple, added a stitch. But that has stopped happening as well. It's as though everyone else has become a disconnected stranger.

"At the risk of sounding melodramatic, I'm fairly sure I'm dead. There's not much that can be done about it now, but I would like to understand how it happened, and who it was, or simply what it was, that killed me. Was it an enemy, or a lover? A lover who'd become an enemy? Was it some fatal knowledge, a glimpse of insight that finishes off whatever you'd been before?

This city? A suicide for all I know? And what am I supposed to do now, being dead and yet stuck here?"

So that he doesn't reply too quickly, Vojacek makes himself take a slow swallow of the beer that just arrived, and then a second; he lights a cigarette and sucks its first smoke back through his nostrils. (I also paused at this moment for a quick detour through the internet, where I learned that delusions of death and delusions of immortality occur at roughly equal rates and both go by the same name, Cotard's syndrome.) "I read recently," Vojacek resumed after a slow exhale, "about a Romanian fellow who, after having gone missing for many years, returned home to discover he'd been declared dead by the state, at the request of his wife, his ex-wife. Although he was, or at least would seem to be, very much alive, he'd missed the window for appeal, and thus there was nothing more to be done about it; so far as the state, and his widow, were concerned, he was dead."

"I suppose there is some parallel," she acknowledges, "but this is not a bureaucratic matter."

"No," Vojacek agrees, "it isn't."

✢ ✢ ✢

Over the four hundred pages that follow, *Under the Raven* winds through what it might be instead. At times, it reads like a relatively straightforward crime story, with Vojacek easily filling the archetype of a hard-boiled detective and Eva, that's her name, a damsel in distress, but at various turns it suggests instead a political thriller, a hero's journey, a middle-age romance, or a religious allegory. He follows clues, turns a cynical eye on the various suspects, and becomes entangled with the uninventive, literal-minded police. Soon it's revealed that Eva's ex-husband, a deceitful cad, is an ideologue for a clandestine nationalist movement, and through him Vojacek stumbles upon a plot to sabotage the upcoming elections, but that plotline crumbles away as well. (For all their practiced bluster, the aspiring fascists prove too incompetent to pull off more than a random street brawl, largely among themselves, which Vojacek narrowly escapes, winded and dizzy.) He meets colleagues, ex-lovers, the regulars at her corner café, her doctor, a childhood friend, each of whom offers a slightly different, incomplete, and often conflicting image of Eva.

Eva's sister, a calligrapher transcribing Dante's *Divine Comedy* into an ideogram, insists Eva was always hysterical. Outside her studio, while rubbing another cigarette butt into the cobblestones with his leather heel, Vojacek eyes a street urchin studying him from the shadow of an alley. Once she's captured his attention, she backs into a dark recess and the chase is on, although that may be a poor word for it. Only a child, the girl could outrun him at any time; it is less the case that he is chasing her than that she is luring him deeper into the city, through twisting streets, up fire escapes, down tenement hallways, beneath a bridge, through a bank, through a brothel, an art gallery. Each time he nearly loses her, she waits, and he gets some glimpse of her face, a moment of partial recognition. As she turns at the top of a subway entrance, he starts to wonder if the girl might be Eva's child. As though she had been waiting for him to put the clues together, she catches his eye and then disappears.

On a high floor of a dilapidated socialist housing project, he finds Eva's mother in an apartment utterly devoid of personal effects — no photographs, no books, no knitted pillows or mismatched mugs. Her house slippers look virtually unworn. When they talk about Eva, he thinks she might cry but she never does. Wedged into the frame of the mirror by the door there is an unsigned, unsent postcard of Knossos. Anxiously, she ushers him out. Walking down from the apartment (the lift is broken), Vojacek fears his heart is going to give out. On the ground floor, it does. The sky spirals around him and he collapses in the street. When he wakes in a hospital, Eva is beside him.

✣ ✣ ✣

Josef Matousek, the author of *Under the Raven*, worked for several decades as a homicide detective in Prague, and in his author photo he looks, with a barrel chest and olive-green felt blazer, his thin hair greased down and back, more like a midlevel Soviet apparatchik than either a late existentialist or a playful postmodernist. He has a powerful, nut-cracking jaw. He sports the expressionless gaze of someone who already knows what you will say, who even when you lie will know the truth behind your words. He achieved, apparently, brief celebrity in the last decade of the twentieth century for solving the murder of a well-known industrialist with ties to Boris Yeltsin's fast-crumbling regime; his elusive, ironic interviews made him a favorite of the local papers. His colleagues were quite surprised to learn that after he left them, woozy and exposed from drink, he returned to his apartment and wrote. And that when he wrote, he wrote things that, for all their hard-boiled artifice, had about as much logical consistency as an over-easy egg.

For example, take this Vojacek monologue, which sounds like a stand-in for his creator:

> *"Through my many years working as a detective, I started to suspect that the difference between life and death is less absolute than a coroner is trained to perceive. There are living people who carry a bit of death along with them wherever they go — not some inevitable, final moment, but something that permeates their every day; something contagious and gray, played by an out-of-tune violin. And the opposite is even more true — dead people who continue to walk beside us in the evenings, who materialize in the passing windows of trams and subways, who shake their heads, slowly, when we are false, who tug at our sleeves when we try to change.*
>
> *"And some people, well, they drift so endlessly back and forth between the two, who can really tell?*
>
> *"Eventually it came to a head when I was asked to solve a murder my colleagues insisted had happened just days or weeks ago, but which I was convinced had occurred years or even decades earlier. There is never any shortage of suspects. Once you start to think this way, we're all killers.*
>
> *"Having crossed that line, I became very bad at my job and my superiors decided it was best to make a change."*

✢ ✢ ✢

As Vojacek convalesces in the hospital, weaving in and out of consciousness, Eva stays beside him and the narrative imagination of *Under the Raven* shifts from his speculative mind to her more disciplined attention. She worries about his health and half suspects, despite the obvious evidence of tobacco-stained fingers and broken blood vessels around his nose, despite the sagging, puffy eyes, that it has been her presence that has somehow infected him with the death she's been carrying around, that she has given it to him.

This suspicion is particularly gnawing and guilt-ridden in that she, while he sleeps, sometimes leaves the hospital to walk the streets or find a cup of coffee, and she begins to feel something stirring within her, something spring-like, a lightness that isn't ghostly. She is able to think not just about her past and the mistakes she made, not just about the splintering tracks, but also about what might actually come next. There is a spa town she remembers, a place where she had a brief but lingering romance many years ago, and a long chapter spools through that history. Maybe, she thinks, mountain air would do her good, that, for the first time in years, good could be done. She notices she's humming. What would he, this troubled and wounded knight, think — what would he say — if she invited him to escape with her?

The end is a bit confusing, which might be tied to a clumsy translation, or perhaps Matousek himself was losing interest in his own story line, or maybe he was grasping for one more moment of blurred possibilities. In any case, although Eva has little appetite, out of some lingering habit she's ordered a decadent chocolate mousse alongside her cappuccino, and with slow bites she lets its bitter richness dissolve on her tongue. It's midmorning and the café sits elevated half a floor above the sidewalk, allowing her to look down on the passersby. (Is she, for example, meant to be in heaven, looking down upon us, or has she reentered the world?) There is a group of men in their blue overalls with lunch pails and camaraderie, and a pack of university students, boys and girls both, flirting and aimless. There is a serious woman, who might be the bearer of bad news, an accusation, an escort to the end, coming steadily toward her, as true death always does. *Keep walking, keep walking,* Eva says to herself, and the woman does, straight beneath Eva's gaze and finally out of sight. Her hand shaking ever so slightly, Eva lifts the spoon back to her lips where the chocolate tastes sweet.

THE SOUTH AFRICAN WRITER IVAN VLADISLAVIC IMAGINED what he called a "loss library," a kind of heavenly space preserved for a collection of perfect books that were never actually written. There are many reasons why. Because their authors — John Keats, Bruno Schulz — died too young, or were swallowed up by monstrous events. Because their authors were discouraged before they even began. Because their authors squandered whatever talents they had and were unable to finish, or because their authors spoke too much and wrote too little. Because these books were based upon the most astonishing, revealing dreams, and the dreams were all but forgotten upon waking. While the loss library gives these unwritten works to the world, its caveat is that none of the books can actually be touched or read. They are to remain permanently on the shelves, guarded by a beautiful and severe librarian.

✢ ✢ ✢

Coiling and Recoiling: An Anthology of Anthro-Reptilian Eroticism
Shikha Sen

In classical versions of *Leda and the Swan*, whether rhymed by Ovid or carved in marble by a Renaissance master, a lusty Zeus assumes the form of a pure white, elegant bird that seduces, or possibly rapes, Leda. This iconography is now so deeply ingrained in our cultural consciousness that it is virtually impossible, for me anyway, to hear the name Leda without simultaneously imagining a long neck and a violent flutter of snowy feathers.

But at an earlier time, other versions of this tale flourished that have since been forgotten, if not forcibly removed from the canon. In one, attributed to the Greco-Alexandrian poet Meleager, Zeus transforms himself not into a web-toed Romeo but a large, muscular crocodile who lures, through the slow pulsing of his nostrils and his watery eyes, an Egyptian princess, on the morning of her wedding day, into the warm marsh grasses along the Nile, and in that rich, fertile, sucking mud they beget Helen, whose beauty is so extreme it will spark a ten-year war and the destruction of a great city and many royal families, as well as one of the greatest stories ever told.

✥ ✥ ✥

The Gnostic codices discovered in Nag Hammadi near Luxor in Upper Egypt in 1945 have upended many assumptions about early Christian orthodoxy. Among the fifty-three texts is one titled "The Third Treatise of the Great Seth," which retells our expulsion from Eden. According to the Great Seth, Eve and a lizard, with four limbs and a tail, lived together rapturously in the Garden in the infinite time before Time, entwined and complete. But made reckless by their incessant coupling, they persuaded one another to seize God's wisdom, which manifested itself in the form of an apple. For their transgression, the lizard was stripped of his appendages and sentenced to slither through muck and weeds for all eternity on his scaled belly.

Poor Eve was punished by being made the wife of the dull ape Adam with his heavy hands and unflickering tongue.

✧ ✧ ✧

The early medieval legend of Saint George and the dragon revolves around a Libyan kingdom terrorized by a horrible lizard that has demanded the king's daughter as his bride. Distraught, the impotent locals prepare to oblige, but at the last moment dashing, blond, and blue-eyed Saint George arrives and bests the beast, which he drags back to the king's feet and beheads. The people are so awed by George's feat that they convert to Christianity on the spot and accept baptism. As the story spread, Saint George became an icon of courtly love, inspiring knights to the heights of chivalry, resulting in generations of abducted daughters being rescued back and forth from varied keeps.

There was also, however, an apocryphal version of the story that circulated throughout the Middle Ages in which the princess is not sacrificed to the dragon but elopes with it, and in which Saint George is not celebrated as a proto-Aryan hero but derided as a patriarchal enforcer sent to restore dominion and control over a community set free by an unspeakable lust. Prized manuscripts of this version, illuminated with rich purple inks drawn from the glands of Mediterranean snails and lapis lazuli from the hills of Afghanistan, were known to pass in secret through nunneries of North Africa and Syria.

✥ ✥ ✥

I found each of these and many other curiosities in Shikha Sen's *Coiling and Recoiling: An Anthology of Anthro-Reptilian Eroticism*, a textbook-like volume with a thick, almost cardboard cover glazed with an image of the Creature from the Black Lagoon carrying a scantily-clad, pertly-breasted woman — terrified, but perhaps excited too — back to his lair and probably not for his next meal.

In her introduction, Sen confesses:

Other than the two Dippers, Orion's Belt, and the Southern Cross, I am utterly incapable of recognizing constellations in the night sky, which not only disappoints me but feels counter to my sense of self. Or at least counter to my sense of aspired self. If I were the person I wished to be, that I sometimes persuade others I am, I'd wander dark fields at night, beach cliffs, abandoned cities, and see the sky a-swirl with bandits and scorpions and octopi and great ships. Around campfires, I'd tell their tales. But instead: countless disassembled pricks of light.

Is this a consolation? I rarely wander dark fields at night, beach cliffs, or abandoned cities, but I do often meander around my home, from shelf to shelf, pausing by my desk or bedside to leaf though the books stacked there, and sometimes I feel like I can begin to glimpse, or at least contrive, amongst the varied metaphors and plots the outline of some larger theme taking form not within a single volume but across many.

And what is this secret pattern Sen claims to have recognized? A persistent strain of "anthro-reptilian eroticism." Misquoting Jung, she proposes: "The lizard shows the way to hidden things and expresses the introverting libido, which leads man to go beyond the point of safety, and beyond the limits of consciousness . . ."

What brought Sen to this realization was New Directions Publishing's reissue of Rachel Ingalls' *Mrs. Caliban*, a novella about a distressed housewife's affair with a lizard-like creature, Larry, who has escaped from a research facility and taken shelter in her home. Unlike her philandering husband, Larry is a kind soul who longs to make frequent love, eat avocados, and return to his people. At virtually the same time, inspired by either zeitgeist or plagiarism, Guillermo del Toro released *The Shape of Water*, a movie in which a mute cleaning woman falls in love with a humanoid sea creature who, Larry-like, is being subjected to cruel tests in a secret lab. There is no husband in her home, but the lab is governed by a sadistic overseer.

As Sen pondered the concurrence of these two very odd and yet very similar tales, she remembered something else altogether, the novel *Cold Skin* by the Spaniard Albert Sánchez Piñol, which describes a man who has been sent to staff a lighthouse on the edge of the Antarctic Circle. (Oulipian challenge: write a story in which a lighthouse keeper is not deranged.) In the darkest hours of a sunless winter, the lighthouse is besieged by a horde of bipedal, frog-like sea creatures who emerge from the icy waters with murderous intent, or at least with hearty appetites. In the struggle that ensues, the hero captures one of the creatures, a female, whom he domesticates and eventually takes as a lover, an uncomfortable and probably not at all accurate phrase. (Although unmentioned by Sen, Piñol's next novel, *Pandora in the Congo*, while set in Africa rather than the frozen south, follows virtually the same plot, with a pair of explorers discovering a mysterious cave in the lost heart of the jungle that seems to lead to the center of the earth, and that houses a terrifying mass of reptilian humanoids, including one that becomes the hero's erotic interest. His third-best-selling, and least interesting, book is about the fully human siege of Barcelona.)

As Sen began to draw a line between *Mrs. Caliban* and *Cold Skin*, she thought of an additional coordinate, "Spar," a short story by Kij Johnson about a woman who has narrowly escaped an accident in deep space that killed her husband, only to be rescued from oblivion by a passing ship, which is hardly large enough for its sole passenger, a cool-skinned, elusively formed, boneless, muscular, slimy blob. As she grapples with her grief, she also grapples with the alien's many tentacles, which are intent on probing her nose, ears, mouth, anus, and vagina. "She penetrates it, as well."

Tonally, they are utterly different tales. *Mrs. Caliban* reads almost like a parody of a *Ladies' Home Journal* story; *Cold Skin* is gothic and erotized; "Spar" is sparse, wounded, and brutal. But they all hinge around a similar, transgressive act: sex, or something very close to it, with lizard-like creatures. And in each case, it is this transgression that allows a maimed person to reclaim their humanity.

Sen continues:

At first, I assumed that Ingalls, Piñol and Johnson — del Toro, too — were reacting against the drift of our cultural imagination toward a world of perfectly formed, pleasure-providing, submissive androids. What J. D. Ballard called "the body's dream of becoming a machine." Rebelling against this sterile fantasy, they were seeking out one rooted in the deep, hungry pulsing of our brainstem.

As I continued to read, however, I began to sense that there was something timeless in this alternative fantasy of lizard love, something that had been slithering through our collective subconscious for hundreds of generations. Once I allowed myself to recognize this passion wasn't merely a momentary reaction to a modern predicament, I began to hunt down its antecedents.

The balance of his book, rolling out in binary chapters that include "Women Abducted by Lizards" and "Women Who Abducted Lizards," "Marriage" and "Sudden Couplings," "Men Who Rode Dragons" and "Dragons Who Rode Men," is an assembly of the research that followed, in European monasteries and libraries, in the far reaches of the internet, and at varied used bookstores and chat rooms.

✢ ✢ ✢

One additional discovery: Like his cousin Odysseus, the Baghdadi sailor Sinbad inspired both a great epic and countless variants that have woven in and out of his mythology as he has traveled not just over the seas but through our centuries. In one largely forgotten but once popular version from the sixteenth century, Sinbad encounters a race of mermaids off the coast of Somalia. Unlike their European cousins, these mermaids were not female above, fish below, but slim, slippery humanoid creatures, covered in scales with cartilaginous ridges or fins down the center of their backs; thick, twitching tails; and unusually long, jointless fingers. In an adventure forgotten in, or possibly purged from, the later editions, Sinbad is seduced by their queen, who teaches him how to navigate by stars as he travels over the equator into the Southern Hemisphere, a metaphor in the caliphate, apparently, for the knowledge that can be gained as we pass beyond the human norm.

THE AMERICAN WRITER RICHARD BRAUTIGAN IMAGINED a library of unpublished, perhaps unpublishable, manuscripts, on any subject whatsoever and assembled without order. "It doesn't make any difference where a book is placed because nobody ever checks them out and nobody ever comes here to read them," he wrote. "This is not that kind of library. This is another kind of library." Eventually in his honor just such a library was created in Vermont.

✤ ✤ ✤

The Threaded Trail
Amalia Delicari (trans. Maria Kodama)

At my first attempt to open Amalia Delicari's *The Threaded Trail*, I was surprised by the book's resistance. The cheap glue used to adhere its eight bound sections to the frail spine had hardened, either at once or perhaps over the many years the book stood neglected and pressed between two others. When *The Threaded Trail* finally gave, it did so with an audible crack. To loosen the pages, I bent them far back to the right and then let them roll out from under my thumb several times, each pass a little smoother than the last.

The story itself was quite easy to enter, in part because I, like most readers I suspect, was well-acquainted with its beginning. Having lost a war, defeated Athens is now obligated to send seven of its finest young men and seven of its finest young women every seven years to victorious Crete, where something monstrous is ahoof. The Cretan king Minos and his clever adviser Daedalus have built an impossible labyrinth winding through caves and tunnels beneath the palace. It is said to house the Minotaur, a creature with the body of a powerful man and the head and horns of a bull. This is the child of Minos' wife, Pasiphaë, who must have betrayed him with some god or animal. Once the Athenians are delivered, they are stripped naked and forced into the labyrinth, never to be seen again.

By chapter two, fourteen years have passed and yet another offering is required. Theseus, son of the Athenian king, insists on a place among his sacrificed countrymen and women, although he has no intention of dying. He'll kill the beast, he assures his father, and set his people free. Minos, begetter of girls, who has seen both his power expand and his rule become increasingly corrupt and violent, welcomes this prince — handsome, iron-like, and oiled — into his household and insists that on the boy's last night he dine alongside the royal family. There, Minos' youngest daughter, Ariadne, falls hopelessly in love.

In the late hours of night, she sneaks into Theseus' chamber and promises to help him, an offer that he, with all the bravado of youth, finds amusing. He is perfectly confident in his own abilities, certain of victory. But when she unrolls a cloth to reveal a sword, a torch, and a spool of golden thread, he grows more attentive. She leads him to the labyrinth's entrance, a set of lichen-crusted stairs winding down into the darkness.

For hours he wanders through the corridors as they divide and multiply, past scattered bones, some broken and discarded, others stacked ceremoniously. As he walks, he unspools the thread behind him. Many of the walls are scratched, perhaps by the creature's claws; the deeper he goes, guided by the torch's unsteady light, the more these marks begin to resemble signs and images. Perhaps a herd of cattle? A winged man circling the sun? A school of dolphins comforting a lone ship? This Theseus, however, is not the interpretive type, and rather than reading clues he marches onward.

Finally, at the heart of the labyrinth, he discovers the Minotaur — who snorts and swings his heavy head from side to side, who charges and impales Theseus against a wall with one of his great horns, extinguishing him on the spot. Pushing a hoofed foot against the wall, the Minotaur frees himself and the dead boy slumps to the ground.

As the Minotaur stands panting over the lifeless body, all the rage and adrenaline this unexpected encounter has awoken in him slowly dissipates, and he begins to sense something else, an unsteady weakness spreading through his limbs, dizziness, nausea. He drops to a single knee. He's killed before, many times, but something different has happened here, something to himself. He crawls to a pool of water to wash the blood from his hands and rinse his mouth. There in the dim, rippled reflection he watches as his horns dissolve and his face transforms into one that at first seems merely human but that he soon recognizes as belonging to the stranger he just killed. With fine, royal fingers, he strokes his hairless chin. He blinks. He's become so attuned to the darkness that the dim glitter of a golden thread catches his eye. Stumbling at first, he follows it back through the labyrinth. As he climbs the stairway up and to its opening, the sun, which he hasn't seen for a lifetime, is just beginning to rise. It blinds him, and he nearly collapses back into the labyrinth, but a woman rushes forward and embraces him, weeping with joy. By her scent, he recognizes his own kin.

Dazed, disoriented, he's led down to the docks where Ariadne has secured the Athenian ship with a small crew to provide them and Theseus' thirteen compatriots safe passage home. They push off into the surf. By the time drums and warning bells roil the Cretan shore, they are curling over the horizon, their sails billowing with wind. That night, in the ship's cabin, she seduces him, and afterward, as they lie side by side, she begs him to tell her how he killed the dreaded beast, to describe its horrible limbs and face, how it suffered its rightful end. Eventually he dozes off and sleeps restlessly. The following day they set anchor at Naxos to fill their barrels with fresh spring water, and he realizes that these people, *his* people, will do whatever he asks of them. Before dawn, he orders them to silently reload the ship and depart, abandoning his sister to her fate.

When Theseus had left Athens, he'd promised his father that if he succeeded in killing the Minotaur, his ship would return flying a white sail as a signal of victory, but the Minotaur-as-Theseus is ignorant of this pact, and his ship enters the Athenian harbor under its standard black wing. When Theseus' father, who watches every day from the cliffs for his son's unlikely return, sees this banner of defeat, he throws himself into the sea in despair. After seven days of mourning, Theseus is crowned the king of Athens. His childhood friends and the varied princes, the castle's courtiers and ladies note, in their varied ways, how he's changed, grown more remote and hardened, but that is easily attributable to a son's grief at his father's death and the grand responsibilities he has now been asked to assume.

After this diversion from the common tale, Delicari returns for several chapters to a string of events — vanquishing drunken centaurs, venturing into Hades — that constitute the life of Theseus as it has been told by Sophocles, Ovid, Plutarch, Chaucer, Racine, Renault, and others. But she also layers two additional stories into these legends.

As its king, Theseus elevates Athens from a vulnerable outpost to Attica's dominant city-state, and Delicari records not just his victories in battle, but also how he begins a tradition of patronage for the arts and letters, building theaters and schools of philosophy, welcoming sophists into the city's forum for lively debates. While his renown comes from acts of heroism and strength, it is in these games — the twisting logic of public debate, the elusive words declaimed on a stage — that the Minotaur is able to imagine himself, for even a few moments, free again in the elegant and nurturing labyrinth of his youth. He takes a bull's head as his icon, and the backside of Athens' golden coins are stamped with a maze, which his people think honors his first victory, but which represents to him his enduring kingdom.

In her final chapter, roles have been thoroughly reversed. Athens is now ascendant and Crete a subjugated state. Its elderly queen, Pasiphaë (Minos' wife; he is long dead) arrives to pay homage to Theseus and ask for his mercy as he sets the terms of their surrender. But she is a proud woman and unable to play the part of supplicant to a man she believes killed her only son, monster or not, and who disgraced and abandoned her daughter. Rather than humbling herself, she provokes and insults Theseus, who "snorts" in disgust, a sound so unnatural or at least inhuman that it startles her into silence.

Staring into the king's cold eyes, their irises ringed in yellow, she has a terrible moment of recognition. Startling the courtiers and sycophants who fill the chamber, she stands and, trembling, approaches the king, who recoils from her withered touch, but with both hands she combs through his hair, thumbing the curve of his skull from which his great horns once rose, before dropping to her knees to kiss his rough and calloused toes.

Quite a few science fiction writers have imagined ultimate libraries, collections that bring together every book ever written or even, in some cases, every book that ever will be written. More rigorously, THE ARGENTINE WRITER JORGE LUIS BORGES IMAGINED a rigidly geometric, nearly infinite library that contains every possible book created through the random combination of twenty-three letters and precisely 410 pages. They are mostly senseless, impenetrable tombs, but just as a tiny speck of life ever so rarely manifests among billions of stars, so too an occasional work of literature assembles itself out of this scattering of letters — *an Odyssey, a Divine Comedy*.

✢ ✢ ✢

Six-Legged Stars
Sylvia Armentrout

The cover image of Sylvia Armentrout's *Six-Legged Stars* is an extreme close up of an ant's face. It is a terrifying sight — hard, scarred, brutal, and focused. As much a battering ram as animal. Or a fierce rock. Its mouth seems almost stitched shut, crisscrossed by a series of ... I'm not quite sure what. Hairs? Needles? I'm grateful it can't smile.

It is a well-suited image for the book, which takes us down to the level of the ant, the fly, the bedbug, the wasp, and to see the world from their vantage. Here are a few things I read in Armentrout's pages:

That the emperor moth emerges from its cocoon with magnificent wings and delicate antennae but devoid of a mouth, and thus all the labor of metamorphosis produces an elegant creature only able to survive for a brief while on the lipids she stored within her caterpillar-self long, long ago.

That army ants build nests dangling from tree limbs, complete with honeycombed chambers and nurseries, in which every joist and structure, every rafter and beam, every gateway and bridge is constructed from the living, twisting bodies of the ants themselves and reflecting some primordial instinct of city.

That leafcutter ants feed exclusively on a fungus they cultivate in farms buried deep within their vast excavated colonies. They can take no other nourishment.

That the botfly is too clumsy to lay its eggs directly on a human, chimpanzee, or gibbon host, and thus adheres its eggs to the bellies and limbs of captured mosquitoes, who are better designed to penetrate primate defenses.

Colin Hamilton

That the seventeen-year cicada survives all those years buried in the ground by penetrating a passing root with his rostrum, a sharp, hollow needle that extends from his chest, and slowly nourishing himself on the flowing sap.

That pairs of Asian wood-eating cockroaches enforce their monogamous relationships by gnawing off one another's wings.

✤ ✤ ✤

But, honestly, most of that I already knew. I've read many insect books like *The Infested Mind: Why Humans Fear, Loathe, and Love Insects* (Jeffrey A. Lockwood), *The Fabulous Insects* (Charles Neider, editor), *Insect Mythology* (Gene Kritsky and Ron Cherry), *Insectopedia* (Hugh Raffles), and *Inherit the Earth* (Arjun Gupta).

What makes Armentrout's book a lost treasure is that she is not actually an entomologist or even a science journalist, but something I would classify instead as a moralist. A moralist more interested in insects than her fellow humans. I should have known given that the book doesn't open with a quote from E.O. Wilson or his kind but from Aesop: "We may often be of more consequence in our own eyes than in the eyes of our neighbors."

Thus we also learn:

That "cicada biology has evolved over millions of years to accommodate a large, empty, and resonant chamber that might, in a different universe, have been filled instead by powerful muscles, fine spools of silk, stinking tar, or deadly poison, but that has been left hollow like a natural chapel through which the cicada can bellow and hum its droning song of being."

That disorder is the nature of the universe. For example, leafcutter ant cities are under perpetual assault from bees and wasps, marauding antlions, beetles and roaches, and hairy, wine-dark tarantulas. She writes:

At some point, this season or after a hundred generations have been born and died, their city's defenses inevitably collapse and all will appear lost. At that moment, a sisterhood of would-be queens will fill their jaws with samples of the eternal, life-giving fungus — like monks and scholars fleeing a burning city with a few books hidden in their robes — and take flight, beginning the quest for a new Byzantium.

As for the praying mantis:

Some creatures are so adept at killing they can do little else. All the achievements of society — politics and art, history and science — are lost to them; any notion of companionship a threat. The Greeks called her 'the prophet,' but of what? Only death. With her flexible neck, the mantis can rotate her head in a wide pivot, fixing her singular, hypnotic gaze on any extinguishable pulse of life troubling her presence. Crickets, grasshoppers, dragonflies — their frantic struggles are useless once seized by the mantis' terminal talons; nothing escapes. Holding tight, the mantis calmly presses her prey's head down and devours it from the back of the neck.

Even insects as large as herself — and of her own kind, her own family — are hunted, with the mantis stretching her terrible, flayed wings, rising high on her legs, piercing talons held still higher. Even the biological necessity to mate is tinged with a deadly thrill, ritualized and dramatic. The male — the smaller, weaker male — will approach a female cautiously. He'll bow his head in submission to her, to fate, then erect his wings and display his thorax. Compelled and reluctant, he'll mount her back. Once they are locked together, he'll cling desperately to her for five or six hours. Afterward, as sometimes happens, she turns and eats his head.

Armentrout tells a terrifying story of a "larval bee grown fat and dull from an excess of honey." Her aunts weave her within a many-layered cocoon where she will remain "in a suspended dream, entirely obliviously to the storms and seasons and passing fox until she is ready to emerge and take her place among the colony." But then, "like the first inkling of a nightmare," a tiny white worm, emerging half-formed out of the nothingness, discovers her shelter and begins to patiently explore its architecture, seeking out any crack that opens a narrow path through the layers of hardened silk. While her cocoon may be an impenetrable to the powerful wasp or deadly spider, it is an irresistible lure to this simple worm who is guided through the labyrinthine weaving by the warmth of the dreaming bee.

At the end of his journey, he simply lies exhausted beside her at first. Although he had been engineering to slither and seek, he is mouthless and, in his present state, incapable of eating. Armentrout:

But change is the nature of things, and through the long night he begins to transform himself from what he'd been — smooth, legless, white, blind, and hungry — into another worm. He still has no mandibles, piercers, or teeth with which to consume, and possibly stir, the larval bee, but he adheres his primitive lips to her side and begins to slowly leach, over days and even weeks, all the liquid from the sleeping bee, who is drained into a stillborn shell.

Armentrout claims the walking stick's biological viability is:

... predicated on his ability to appear like something he is not — on his willing, total forgoing of self. Only by submitting to his arboreal anonymity can he survive; any impulse toward individuality or expression, a single moment of honesty, is fatal, for he has no other defense. This submission is so complete that sometimes a single walking stick will come to imagine himself to actually be a twig, which sparks a deep confusion when other twigs around him never move, never inch toward a soft, chewable leaf, never respond to the essential but fatal urge to procreate. Perhaps he watches those others, those truer twigs with a sense of admiration or envy even, those who have fully become what he only aspires to be. Tense and hopeful, he watches a robin land beside him and pluck a twig in its beak to be carried high into the trees and woven purposefully into its nest.

Colin Hamilton

For Armentrout, the existence of a green darner dragonfly revolves around a simple dilemma: the more he consumes, the faster he grows, and as he grows, his surging inner self must struggle against the hard, fixed shell that encapsulates him. The eternal battle between what we are and what we might become. Finally, the pressure is too great and the emerging beast cracks through its casing to reveal something new and different. This process begins at birth and repeats itself over and over; by the fourth molt, the dragonfly's wing buds are beginning to form, and his adolescent body has stretched longer and stronger. She writes:

> *Only the hunger stays the same, only that eternal ache, and eventually it compels the adolescent dragonfly to crawl up his weeds and out of the water that has sheltered his larval existence, out into the cool, open air. Once more a cleft begins to open while the dragonfly quivers on a reed, splitting the skin first behind his head, cracking both backward and forward as he struggles against it, pushing through, at last, as a fully formed adult: slimmer, iridescent, birdlike. He has six thin, spiny legs but is too weak to take a single step. There is a black spot ringed by blue and then yellow crowing his forehead. His large, compound eyes rotate, absorbing the world through hundreds of fragments. Panting beside his abandoned shell, he is helpless and soft until the sun, which he'd known only as a dull glimmering beneath the water, can dry and harden him.*

How tempting it must be to simply stay like that, finished. But the hunger never abates, never allows a moment of peace. At last, he stretches his wings, meshed and purring, and takes to the air. A lean, ferocious hunter, he'll now spend almost every waking moment circling endlessly above the surface of the pond. With his large, fractured eyes rotating, he takes everything in, every flicker of midge, mosquito. With startling precision and speed, he'll swoop down to snare his prey in perpetual quest for the energy needed to keep his wings' thoracic muscles in motion.

As the green darner dragonfly grows and masters both his wings and horrible jaws, he'll learn to take his hunt higher into the realm of damselflies, the self-absorbed butterflies, and even lesser members of his own tribe, anything that might momentarily fill the insistent void at his core. But the more exulted he climbs, the closer this Icarus comes to his own inevitable demise: the sparrows, kites, and kingfishers that command and terrorize the true skies.

THE AMERICAN WRITER A. J. HACKWORTH IMAGINED a library that serves as a repository for as-yet-unwritten books. More specifically, for dangerous books its librarians are actively preventing from becoming written. Every so often, one of these embryonic ideas will escape into the world, at which point a librarian is assigned to retrieve this nascent threat before it can find an author and be brought to formidable life.

✢ ✢ ✢

This Is Not a Biography: The Life of David Markson
Jasper De Jong

For comparison, imagine a biography of the artist Yves Klein in which the only color ever referenced but repeated obsessively over hundreds of pages, through his childhood and adolescence, through first loves and triumphs, thinning hair and expanding waistline, was the iconic, ultramarine blue that would become his signature expression. Or a biography of James Joyce written in an imitative style of relentless word play, all allusions and scatological jokes. A biography of Picasso written in shattered, disjointed frames of prose, or better yet a biography of Picasso that discovers a new color palate and style for each chapter. A biography of Alan Turing in which every sentence has the rigorous discipline, the inevitable last word, of the perfect algorithm.

Such logic seems to have inspired Jasper De Jong's *This Is Not a Biography*, a biography of David Markson.

Markson was a famously unfamous New York writer of experimental fiction, whose work culminated a signature style that defined his final four books: *Reader's Block, This Is Not a Novel, Vanishing Point,* and *The Last Novel.* These books, which form a single body of work — *The Notecard Quartet* — are made up of hundreds of brief, often grammatically inverted thoughts and observations, primarily about the lives of other artists. They capture the occasional accomplishment but mostly fixate on their disappointments, neglect, and transience, with the occasional baseball reference interspersed. Each fragment, we are told, is drawn from a box of index cards the author has been assembling for some time, over decades perhaps, and at first they seem randomly clustered, but over the pages certain themes and patterns begin to emerge, tracing unexpected connections across centuries and lives. Deeply elegiac, *The Quartet* is the work of an artist whose own career has been accomplished but not transcendent and whose time is ending quickly, who is seeking to find or claim for himself a place among a pantheon he admires. (Markson's last four novels were published by three different presses, arguably of diminishing consequence and reputation.)

While I recommend all 267 pages, an abridged version of *This Is Not a Biography* could read as follows:

Is there a canon of writers whose dead bodies were found by their ex-wives?

Nobody comes, nobody calls.

Albany, New York, Markson was born in. The same year as Gabriel García Márquez.
Son of a newspaperman and a schoolteacher.

First and foremost, I think of myself as a reader, he would remember Borges writing.

A man will turn over half a library to make one book, Samuel Johnson added two centuries earlier.

Was Markson from the last generation of writers to serve in the military and whose imagination was shaped by baseball?
On a dial radio?

By Malcolm Lowry?

Fitzgerald, by the time he died, had been all but forgotten and soon Gatsby was out of print.

As a young writer Markson wrote to Lowry, asking for his mentorship. Not knowing that Lowry had once written a similar letter to Conrad Aiken.
Which he learned years later, from a urine-stained and homeless Lowry who had commandeered his couch.

Finding the full Borges quote and being surprised to remember that it continues: first as a reader, then as a poet, then as a prose writer.
And used to introduce a book of poetry to an audience that preferred his fictions.

David Markson was not an anti-Semite.
He kept a list of those who were.

All you ever seemed to do down here for three years was drink, but damn it, you were paying attention, a Mexican girlfriend marveled.

Wondering how that entered the historical record.

Markson edited crime fiction for Dell Books in the 1950s. To support his family, he sold entertainments — *Epitaph for a Tramp*, *Epitaph for a Dead Beat*, and *Miss Doll, Go Home*.

As a young father, Markson would sock away money in books. One book for each of his children.

My thoughts were soon crippled if I tried to force them in any single direction against their natural inclination, he explained.

Sold *The Ballad of Dingus Magee; Being the Immortal True Saga of the Most Notorious and Desperate Bad Man of the*

Olden Days, His Blood-Shedding, His Ruination of Poor Helpless Females, & Cetera.
Which underwrote two years in Europe with his family.

An anti-western he called it, nevertheless.

In the movie version, a middle-aged Frank Sinatra played the teenage Dingus.
Or it might have been three.

Going Down, 1970. *Springer's Progress,* 1977.

Rejected fifty-four times, *Wittgenstein's Mistress* was.
Including eight publishers who regretfully called it brilliant.

A tale told by a woman, Kate, who believes herself to be the last person on earth.
The evidence irrefutable. Or at least inescapable. What too much philosophy can do to a person.

Within a year of *Ulysses'* publication, Joyce had lost all of his teeth.

Just forty-one.
Years, that is.

Within two years of its publication, Edmund Gallas opined that there were no English critics of weight or judgment who considered Joyce an author of any importance.

Imagining Markson's pleasure in realizing the New Orleans airport is named for Louis Armstrong and not another third-rate mayor.

Everybody should know even the most obscure painter or composer. But fucking George W. Bush? A hundred years from now? Who will know him any more than they know Chester Alan Arthur? Well, no, it's different, because he may end the world. Said Markson.

Once I had a dream of fame, said Kate.
A problem she solved by being the last person on earth.

Pretty much the high point of experimental fiction this century, said David Foster Wallace.
Solving the need for book blurbs but not healthcare.

Michelangelo slept in his boots, which is a curious detail, but one worthy of mention in four of Markson's books? Eventually they had to be cut from his feet.

Especially when balanced with: No one but Beckett can be quite so funny and sad at the same time as Markson can.
Said Ann Beattie.

Flaubert was more precise, estimating one must read fifteen hundred books to write a single volume.

To write a novel with no intimation of story whatsoever, with no characters. None. Plotless. Characterless. Yet seducing the reader into turning the pages, nonetheless. With a beginning, a middle, and an end. Even a note of sadness at the end.
Markson's aspiration.

What did Markson sleep in?

Napoleon considered Shakespeare unreadable.

Markson considered Wallace Stevens exceeding all twentieth-century American poets in percentage of pure drivel.

Published one novel in the '80s. Published one novel in the '90s. Thin ones.

While filling two shoebox lids with three-by-five-inch cards on the history of art. The places of birth and causes of death. Changing fortunes and swings of reputation. The names of artists whose work he'd leave behind in a burning building if it allowed him to rescue a cat instead, starting but not ending with Julian Schnabel.
The essentials grains filtered through the encyclopedia of time.

How many centuries until no one knows that Keats and Yeats were pronounced differently?

A continued heap of riddles. A treatise on the nature of man. A comedy of sorts. A kind of verbal fugue. A disquisition on the maladies of the life of art. *A novel*.

A perpetual thought-reviser.

In all honesty, I'd spent about an hour rereading some Zbigniew Herbert, and then stop to look up something in this year's *Who's Who in Baseball*, and the next thing I knew I was reading that for just as long.

An assemblage. Nonlinear. Discontinuous. Collage-like.

How many cards fill a shoebox lid? Two thousand? Three?
But what size where Michelangelo's feet?
Stumped.

Quotes without quotations. Anecdotes without attribution.
True because they are true, not because some footnote says so.

Wrote letters on plain white postcards, Markson did, to avoid rambling on.

Was over sixty by the time he became well known for being unknown.

A review of *Vanishing Point*, in the *New York Times*, accidently retitled it *Vanishing Act*.

Or, the best not famous writer in America.
Ann Beattie added.

Flaubert published twelve major works.

Yet not without notoriety. Remembered by a select set as a stud lover-boy cocksman, because he was literary, witty, handsome, and hung.
As prematurely eulogized by Alice Denham in *Sleeping with Bad Boys*.

Wondering which review pleased him more, Wallace's or Beattie's?
Denham's?

Petrarch sometimes wrote letters to long-dead authors.

Markson would call dead friends to listen to ghosts on their answering machines.

Eighteen thousand.

I hate to admit it, and I don't really understand it, but it's some years now — it just seems to have gone dead for me. Not just recent stuff, but even novels that I've deeply cared about, I try to reread and there's none of the reaction I used to get, none of the aesthetic excitement or whatever one wants to call it, all a blank.

The more he wrote, the older he became.

Nobody comes, nobody calls.

Read by students who not only haven't used a typewriter but actually call them typing machines.

With one exception of course. I can always reread Ulysses. But hell, that's not like reading a novel, it's more like reading the King James Bible.

New York City, David Markson died in.

Bequeathed his book collection to the Strand Book Store, where it has been sold off, piece by piece.

Devotees searching the aisles for a Markson-owned copy, scanning the books for marginalia. A running blog commemorates their findings, the Xs, underlines, the exclamation marks. His signature signature inside a front cover.

What an awful couple of pages, he added to *Mao II*. Bullshit!

RAY BRADBURY, ANOTHER AMERICAN, IMAGINED a future without libraries, or rather in which a few rebellious people become the living equivalent of libraries by memorizing essential texts that would otherwise be lost. His compatriot David H. Keller imagined a library comprised of the jarred brains of a special class of humans who had each been assigned to read a book a day for five years. H. P. Lovecraft imagined a library that gathered scholars, or actually *the consciousnesses of* scholars, from across the eras to write manuscripts for its vast collection. The English writer Terry Pratchett imagined a library governed by an orangutan with three tasks: maintaining silence, enforcing the library's lending policies, and safeguarding the physical laws of the universe.

✢ ✢ ✢

Tortured by Roses
M. K. Suzuki (trans. Finn Winsome)

In the tradition of Marcel Schwob's *Imaginary Lives,* J. Rodolfo Wilcock's *The Temple of Iconoclasts,* and Borges' *A Universal History of Infamy,* Roberto Bolaño's *Nazi Literature in the Americas* contains thirty-one biographical sketches of fictional South and North American writers. They are poets and novelists and playwrights, academics and alcoholics, romantic souls and rejected lovers, pamphleteers, copy editors, and plagiarists. Some are petty criminals. They read Ginsberg, Whitman, and Faulkner. They struggle with their weight and their parents' judgments or indifference, with dissolving marriages, with the onward drift of history and their receding hairlines. In other words, they are absolutely typical in most regards. What sets them apart from most of us is their dark attraction to extreme right-wing politics.

While a single profile might constitute a curiosity, his larger argument becomes clear as Bolaño stacks up this pantheon writer after writer, from Argentina through Canada: there is nothing inherently humanity-embracing about artists. Perhaps, just the opposite: there is a foul seed in the writers' profession — the emotional isolation, the desire for control, the constancy of failure and its resulting accusations, the cult-like followings that amass around mysterious and charismatic figures, the angry excommunication of those who stray from the faith — that neatly feeds into fascist ideology. There is, after all, a thin line between the delicate, petal-plucking cliché of the romantic poet and a creature consumed by spite, set upon by imaginary foes: substitute "Jew" for "editor" or "immigrants" for "readers." All fascists are seeking a kind of restoration of destiny denied, a purification through revenge. And who has a longer list of wrongs to right than a poet?

With only a few unfortunate exceptions, Bolaño's pantheon is also defined by minimal talent and persistent failure. These characters are neglected, unread, and pushed far off to the margins of the literary world. Those who break through, momentarily, are generally savaged by more enlightened reviewers, and thus their greatest successes end up entangled with their most public humiliations. As a result, they are not only monstrous in spirit but also imbued with a kind of impotent pathos; many are at least as pathetic in their rage as they are frightening. The result is frequently a hilarious book that leaves the reader with a deep sense of unease, much like listening to Donald Trump reason.

Reading *Nazi Literature in the Americas*, it is easy to imagine a parallel book written about very real, mostly European fascist and fascist-romanticizing writers who were often quite talented and actually great successes, winning major awards and attracting large readerships, their books perpetually rediscovered by critics seeking to distinguish their art from their lives, or who find, in their art, something that rises above the banality of their milieu — Ernst Jünger, Gabriele D'Annunzio, Ezra Pound, Marinetti, Céline, and Curzio Malaparte to name just a few. One might assume that such an anthology, full of effective race-baiting and calls to the young for their early, heroic deaths, would be a lot less amusing than Bolaño's, but M. K. Suzuki's fictionalized account of Yukio Mishima's final days, *Tortured by Roses*, shows that is not necessarily the case.

Mishima's public persona has been defined by humorlessness, but a gift of Suzuki's novel is to remind us how very funny that can be for everyone else.

Suzuki, as indifferent to subtlety as his subject, begins with a story from Mishima's early autobiographical novel *Confessions of a Mask*, in which as a boy Mishima discovers an image of Saint Sebastian, pierced through and beautiful, in one of his father's art books. He knows nearly nothing about Christianity, but he intuitively understands the radiance of purpose, how suffering makes martyrs glow, and how sacrifice can become a kind of holy eroticism. What else could he do but drop his pants? And thus begins a lifelong and thoroughly documented obsession with masturbation. This story may not be true (not much about Mishima is, right down to the name), but it says more about him than the dull facts of childhood: illnesses, petty humiliations, school prizes. He has nothing but scorn for literalism and its idolization of the ordinary.

While still in his mid-thirties, Mishima emerges as the most respected author in postwar Japan and readers devoured his books. Success and failure are relative terms, and most writers would give their children's kidneys for Mishima's awards and accolades, but he holds himself to different standards. Being read has never really been Mishima's ambition; his work is meant to redeem, and Mishima is increasingly convinced his countrymen are so far gone that not even his books can save them.

Suzuki writes:

The war had humiliated the nation, creating, [Mishima]

believed, a people so ashamed of their collective failure that they could only find solace in individualism and its cheap cult of materialism. He watched them betray their past, and for what? Levi's. A decade later, in a country drunk on prosperity, he has become something of a dangerous joke, better known for his right-wing diatribes and love of all things military than for his novels or plays.

Mishima takes up weightlifting and forms a paramilitary troop, the Tatenokai, although he prefers to call them by their anglicized initials, the "SS," comprised of handsome recruits in tight-fitting, stylized uniforms who, on camping trips, drain and drink one another's blood. In the liberalization of the late 1960s, his extremism is almost guaranteed, or even intended, to alienate his readers.

What the sissy critics fail to grasp is that Mishima has to be physically strong so that he can bear great suffering on their worthless behalf. In Mishima's novels and plays, violent death is the constant reward for his most sympathetic characters, not the meaningfully mundane moments adored by realists. In the most memorable scene of his largely forgettable movie career, he plays an army officer who commits *harakiri* with his young wife after a failed coup attempt. The most discussed book of his middle years is a collection of photographs of a nude Mishima being "tortured by roses." Each of these dramas was another scene stolen from his real work of art: the transformation of a man belittled by the twentieth century into a Hero.

As you might expect from someone who publicly documents his orgasms, Mishima fills his home with photos of himself: with a cigarette and rakishly upturned overcoat collar in New York City; with a mad grimace, waving a samurai sword; making a famous actress laugh. Above his desk, he keeps a framed photograph of himself posed as Saint Sebastian. In it, he is bound by the wrists, hanging from a bough, each taut, greased muscle rippling, the loosely knotted loincloth about to slip below his thin waist. He is pierced by three arrows — in his left armpit (the locus, he tells us, of many of his masturbatory fantasies), just beneath his right ribs, in the crease of muscle curving to his pubis. Each is tastefully shadowed by a thin trickle of blood.

When Bolaño published *Nazi Literature in the Americas*, he was largely a failure himself, which lends a curious sympathy to his profiles, even though his politics could hardly have been more different from those of the thwarted dreamers he portrays. The result is a wonderfully complicated book, with most of the characters refracting back and forth between odious beliefs and endearing dysfunctions. There is a very different dynamic at work in *Tortured by Roses*, where the gap between subject (a Nobel Prize short-lister) and author (a near nobody) is absolute. Suzuki has published (possibly self-published?) only one other work, a short literary memoir from his mid-forties, *Wasted Talent*, which passed virtually unnoticed and is now out of print. If there is in fact any meeting of the minds between the two, it would be that they both want to see Mishima tortured. Thus, inevitably, the end.

Mishima is supposed to be writing *The Decay of the Angel*, the final book in his tetralogy, *The Sea of Fertility,* but his mind keeps wandering. It is a complex saga, weaving together four generations through the dubious algebra of reincarnation, interrupted by long, pedantic, and unconvincing philosophical digressions. In sharp contrast to his earlier works, the first three books have gone largely unread, except by a handful of blood-smelling critics. They'd waited a long time to get their revenge. Although *The Sea of Fertility* was meant to revive Mishima's reputation, he has been passed over for the Nobel Prize in favor of another Japanese author, and now it is unlikely such recognition — the only prize equal to his ambition — will ever come.

One of his favorite lines, since it invariably annoys the Left, is that writers should dress like bankers. (He rarely bothers to attribute it to Thomas Mann, nor does he acknowledge that what he really prefers is dressing like a Milanese general on a balcony.) What the statement means to Mishima, however, is that he is not only an artist but also a professional, and so he'll finish this book, on deadline, even though it bores him; even though he's accepted it will carry him no closer to the Truth. He can tolerate the tedium of finishing *The Decay of the Angel* because he is so pleased by the simple perfection of his next story.

Before resuming work, he jots in his notebook: "There are three things I want from my death. First, it must be painful, so there is no question of cowardice. Second, it must be more perfectly performed than any of my plays, before a large and stunned audience. And third, it must come soon, while I am still young enough to cut a beautiful figure in heaven."

What he also hopes, but doesn't put to paper, is that his death will be a tremendous embarrassment to the Japanese government, still perfecting its postwar pacifism, which wants the world to admire the refinement of the nation's tea ceremonies. He can hear, with satisfaction, the prime minister dismissing his performance as "insane," just as the critics have panned *The Sea of Fertility*. Art isn't meant to coddle politicians.

On the day he finishes *The Decay of the Angel*, he seals it in an envelope addressed to his publisher. In a corner he writes, "Human life is limited, but I want to live forever." There is a knock on his door, a car waiting on the street with four of his student-soldiers. As they drive through the city, he composes spontaneous verses like a Tang poet. The familiar guards at the military base allow him in for an appointment with the general. After the formal introductions, his men seize the unsuspecting commander and issue an ultimatum: Mishima must be allowed to address the troops. The troops are gathered. Mishima makes a grand speech about the decay of the country, the loss of honor and pride. He implores the army to rise up and restore the emperor.

But it's too late: the soldiers laugh and heckle him, make obscene gestures and threats. They are, he recognizes, beyond human words. Having failed, as all heroes inevitably fail, as he too needed to fail, Mishima strips to his waist, kneels. He drives the sword into his gut, drags it across his belly. Suzuki: "Because he is a writer, he can't avoid seeing every opening like a mouth — this is, after all, what he wants to say, what he has always wanted to say." News helicopters circle above. Handsomely, he lifts his best side, the right, to face them and grimaces. Camera lenses glitter in the sun.

When the pain becomes too great, one of his men, a favorite, rises to cut off his head but in the monstrous slapstick Mishima's life has become, the acolyte is overcome by nerves and manages to miss his neck three times in a row.

THE JAPANESE WRITER HARUKI MURAKAMI IMAGINED a library where a young boy is imprisoned and obliged to memorize books, after which his "creamy" brain will be eaten. He escapes.

✢ ✢ ✢

Killing Time
Cesar Alvarez

In blazing yellow, bubbly lettering mostly unused since the 1970s, the cover of *Killing Time* declares its author Cesar Alvarez to be "the future of Central American science fiction." Although the words are in quotes, there is no attributed speaker. His editor, presumably? Or Next Galaxy Guides' publicist? If nothing else, a promise from book to reader that it will not be stingy with either adjectives or emotions. A promise it entirely fulfills. Like countless other genre editions, Alvarez's book is not much larger than one's palm but thick with inexpensive, densely printed, easily smudged pages.

We are ten thousand years into the future when this story begins, or essentially as far ahead of the present moment as the advent of agriculture, the birth of civilization, lies in our past. In this future, humans have long since abandoned Earth and reestablished themselves on Mars. We are told that the exodus from a dying blue planet to a desolate red one was traumatic and devastating, sparking a long Dark Age during which vast amounts of knowledge, technology, and art — including virtually everything that had been preserved digitally — was lost, and exactly what happened then in those fragile first Martian generations and centuries is uncertain and contested. It is known, or at least commonly agreed, that at some point in this traumatic transition the entire human population dwindled to a perilous number. But slowly, over hundreds and then thousands of years, those who survived were able to establish a new civilization and master the barren world they'd inherited, spawning generation upon generation.

Like all cultures, this Martian one has mythologized its past. Legends are told and retold about their phoenix-like rebirth from the burning planet they fled, which on some clear nights can be seen among the stars. Very few objects have survived the transition from one world to another, but those little fragments that did, no matter how inconsequential, are treasured.

(A few skeptics and conspiracy theorists contend that Earth, or an Earth-based history and civilization, is just a fantasy, a kind of cosmic bogeyman used by those in power to compel the behavior of the masses, and that the Martians have always been Martian, and that the dead gray ball twinkling in the sky has always been a dead gray ball.)

Over millennia, as this new Martian civilization steadied itself and reproduced, as it banded together into tribes and nations and then empires, as it passed through religious wars and Renaissance, Industrial, and Information Ages, it eventually achieved the capacity for space travel, but rather than aspiring to seek out distant galaxies or unknown aliens, it concentrates all of its resources on expeditions sent back to Earth. Its people are even more curious about where they came from than where they might go next.

Alvarez's narrative unfolds nearly a century after the first Martian archeologists have returned from a sickly planet prone to sudden storms and ravenous swarms of fist-sized cicadas. Given Alvarez's clumsy style, or perhaps this is an issue of a rushed translation, it is difficult to tell whether this is meant as a joke, an allegory or a proposal, but each of the expedition leaders is defined by a neurological condition, further enhanced by some trimming of the cerebellum, that leaves them incapable of orienting in physical space; they are not just constantly lost but also perpetually surprised — each way they turn, it as though they are entering an entirely new domain. In theory, this makes them hyper observant and the most detailed of mapmakers and record keepers. Every few years now, an expedition arrives back on Mars having excavated some corner of a great, lost city or possibly just a forgotten outpost, a village or asylum, and it brings back a hull of mysteries — a phone book, a high school course catalog, a bronze horseshoe, a statue of a smiling, round-bellied man, a mirror, an ornate, cracked vase, a leather apron, a robotic arm, a telescope, a legal ordinance, a book of poetry, solar panels, an incomplete chess set, a dictionary in a previously unknown language — that need to be deciphered and integrated into this new world's understanding of its past. Nothing is dated after 2349.

On Mars, universities, research institutes, and think tanks are all increasingly organized around the interpretation of Earthen flotsam and jetsam. As more is learned, or at least proposed, about Earth's culture and history, it sparks a schism. Most develop an almost fanatical adoration of anything from their lost home, and they believe that Earth's forgotten truths and knowledge are more authentic and valuable than anything that their degenerate civilization could have created for itself.

For others, Earth is a curiosity at best and a shameless legacy at worst, a failed planet, a disaster they miraculously escaped, and one they should keep escaping. As this Martian subculture pieces together our incessant debates about the consciousness of animals, the right to die, the nature of gender, the transmigration of souls, they dismiss our obsessions as weird and quaint, much as, for example, we are mystified to learn that medieval disputes about the number of angels that can dance on the head of a pin could lead men to kill one another.

A central tenet of this new world's belief about its own past is that as Earth became uninhabitable, humanity had heroically banded together in response to a crisis — ecological or plague-like, possibly both — and abandoned the planet as one people late in the twenty-second century. But as the expeditions become more frequent and skilled, and as their scope reaches beyond the known metropolises, they begin to return with objects that would seem to date from hundreds or even several thousand years later. Martian academics generally dismiss these finds as false leads misdated by overexposure to radiation, or even as outright frauds, but a body of evidence begins to accumulate suggesting that their own understanding of the past is at best fragmentary and perhaps entirely wrong.

The novel ultimately pivots around the discovery of a small but well-preserved human outpost in the foothills of the Himalayas, where the last glaciers trickled long after everything else had grown parched and salted. As it is excavated, archeologists — none of whom develop into true characters, just prototypes: the spiritual seeker, the skeptic, the valiant, Cassandra — come to believe it may have been populated for several millennia, though rarely by more than a few thousand people. This encampment, which included a granary and a goat yard, schools, a hospital, some forum that was perhaps a space for political debate or legal hearings, was centered around a particularly well-preserved building best understood as a library. Within it, these people — who by their own records counted to the year 3666 — had amassed, copied, and protected thousands of books, scientific treatises, ethnographies, and works of art, a collection unlike any yet discovered for its depth and totality. Everything these people believed needed to be saved, either to guide their children into the future or to allow the future to understand who they had been. It takes the archeologists and their linguist peers years to translate the language, which bears only the most superficial resemblance to Earth's older tongues.

While the opening of this treasure trove should be a joyous occasion for Mars and perhaps the spark of a new era of science, philosophy, or art, it comes with a dark lining, for part of what is found in these records is evidence that the exodus from Earth was available only to a privileged few, who fled not just a dying world but also their poorer, darker brothers and sisters, who were abandoned to their oxygen-depleted fates. And just as the Martian world had developed a sophisticated mythology of their lost Earthen past, so too these abandoned Earthers evolved a rich set of beliefs about those who'd left them behind. They wrote epic poetry, tragic plays, and speculative fictions imagining the new world that had been created on Mars, a world of greedy self-interest and hate.

As with the doomed Viking Greenlanders before, the bones of these remote villagers, the guardians of Earthen culture, told the story of malnutrition and how each generation became frailer and more stunted than the one before. In the final recopied editions of their literature, which read more like curses than historic records, it becomes clear that they preserved these documents with the hope that someday they'd be found by the ancestors of those who had abandoned them, and that this new knowledge would take all the pleasure from their world.

Tucked into the back pages of the book was — or, I suppose, *is*, as I've left it there for the next reader — a little scrap of paper on which someone had written with a sharp pencil: "One consequence of working in a library is the realization that everything you think someone else has thought before, and often with more rigor."

THE ITALIAN WRITER UMBERTO ECO IMAGINED a library that sustained a "centuries-old murmuring, an imperceptible dialogue between one parchment and another, a living thing, a receptacle of powers not to be ruled by a human mind, a treasure of secrets emanated by many minds, surviving the death of those who had produced them or had been their conveyors." Its complex, geometric design emerged out of a series of interconnected hexagonal rooms, and it was overseen by a blind librarian, Jorge da Burgos.

✢ ✢ ✢

Further Adventures in the Unknown Interior
Javier Sandoval

Javier Sandoval's *Further Adventures in the Unknown Interior* is the second book in a planned trilogy set during the first century of Spaniards in the Americas; the third was never written. Here is how it begins.

Led by a blowhard buccaneer-for-hire, what will become known to history as the Narváez expedition sets off from Cuba in 1527 with three hundred men to explore the southeastern rim of Florida. At arrival, they shipwreck along the coast. Then things start to go wrong.

They are misdirected by the locals who harass them through swamps and dense wilderness, wounding many and killing a few. Of course, there is no gold. Or, according to the natives they round up and torture, there is gold but always somewhere else, farther inland and away, hidden under the corn bins of the next village over no matter what its impoverished residents say. The Spaniards do, on the other hand, discover alligators, fat snakes, mosquitoes, and tropical fevers. Eventually they have to kill and eat their beloved horses. Their teeth begin to loosen and fall out, along with clumps of hair. When there is no way to bury the dead in all that swampy muck, the men become mutinous.

Their only escape is by sea. Although the maps are uncertain, they know the new Spanish capital in Mexico lies to their west. Using deer hides, tree limbs, stirrups, spurs, and horseshoes, they cobble together five unseaworthy rafts. They knit sails from their shirts and push off into the surf, overloaded with men but shy of either food or fresh water. Their skin burns and bubbles. They stick close to the coast and as best they can to one another, but when they come to the mouth of a monstrous river, its currents sweep them far out into the gulf and apart.

Three of the rafts and all the men they carried are never seen again, but two are caught up in a hurricane that spins them in circles before they capsize on the coast. They call it the Isle of Doom, most likely Galveston Island. There are about eighty survivors, a number that thins to just fifteen over a hard and hungry winter. Come spring, they are taken in by a local tribe that feeds and shelters them, but that also, as weeks become months, puts these uninvited and hungry guests to rough work. With a finely tuned sense of injustice, they think of themselves as slaves. After several slow years pass, there are only four survivors: three Spanish captains — Álvar Núñez Cabeza de Vaca, Andrés Dorantes de Carranza, and Alonso del Castillo Maldonado — and a Moroccan, Esteban, who knows something a little different about bondage, having been brought to this expedition to serve Dorantes.

Certain that they too will die in this wretched land without any priest to bless their souls and absolve the Spaniards' mounting sins, the survivors rally themselves and one night they escape and head west, hoping they can walk their way to Mexico. It is a hard trek, but they care for one another as they go, tending to rashes and the split soles of their feet, to the despair that passes among them like a fever and to which only Esteban seems immune. When the others stumble and collapse, he scavenges enough to keep them nourished and pushes ahead to find fresh water and forge trails. He learns the local languages well and becomes an able intermediary between the Spaniards and the natives, who, they recognize, aren't so much savages as just very different people, capable of kindness and invention.

Across a sparse country, they encounter various clans and subclans, families and cousins. Most are cautiously welcoming, which frequently means they offer to engage with these strangers through trade. Our wanderers, however, have nothing of value to offer, just the same prickly pears and green walnuts everyone gathers. In a moment of desperation, they offer to heal the sick.

At first, they proceed carefully, tending only to those whose ailments are relatively mild and who will probably recover just fine all on their own, but even so the Spaniards feel a certain dread when they're called upon to perform these tasks that bridge physical and spiritual knowledge. They cross themselves and ask for forgiveness. To both their relief and growing unease, they prove to be unexpectedly adept at this work. Before long, their reputation precedes them across the hill country, and they are sought out by various tribes who need their help.

And then something like a miracle occurs. They are brought to a village where a great warrior is dying. An arrowhead has been driven into his shoulder, and the wound festers and burns. His entire arm has turned an angry, swollen red; his fingers are blackening. They try to explain that there is nothing they can do, but his people are insistent, possibly threatening. While the Spaniards dither, Esteban begins praying extravagantly to some god or more likely to the devil, and then he cuts the warrior open. He digs his fingers into the flesh and pushes the stone out through muscle and pus before patching the wound with a paste of mashed herbs. All night Esteban stays by his side, murmuring incantations no one understands, watched closely by the man's brothers and sons. When morning comes, the warrior wakes from his fever, and though he's clearly delirious, he rises to his knees and then his feet before announcing he's been cured. The three Spaniards know this cannot be the work of their Lord, but when a grand meal is served in their honor, they eat ravenously.

Soon an entourage attaches itself to these strange healers, and they are brought fresh deer and fruit as they travel. As they pass from one village to the next, preceded always by their growing reputations and by outlandish hopes, they cure leprosy, tumors, and other ailments.

Nine years after first setting foot in Florida, and more than eighteen hundred miles to the west, they encounter a party of men on horses — Spaniards out rounding up slaves, who are confused when a native party doesn't scatter at their approach. Instead, Cabeza de Vaca, who at this point is hardly distinguishable from his escorts, speaks to them in their own language. After some confusion and storytelling, the wanderers are separated from their native guides and taken to the new world capital to meet the governor, who celebrates both them and his good luck. Although he has his hands full keeping the colony in check, his attention has started to turn away from the tedium of administration, lured by rumors he's begun to hear about a country farther north that is said to include "the Lost Seven Cities of the Portuguese Bishops." It is made entirely of gold, which, after the initial ransacking of the Aztecs, has proved annoyingly elusive to the colonists.

The four men have seen nothing of any wealth on their journey, but over the years they have become more savvy traders, and they are careful in their remarks to keep the vague possibility of lost treasures alive. In gratitude for their rescue and the future it offers, the three Spaniards give Esteban to the governor, suggesting he might be a valuable guide should the governor want to send an expedition north in search of the bishops.

That, a nine-year odyssey across a foreign land, accounts for the first forty-five pages of *Further Adventures in the Unknown Interior*. So far as I know, it is basically true, or true to the historical record. What comes over the following 987 pages is a purely fictionalized account of the four survivors in the aftermath of that grand and nightmarish adventure.

✢ ✢ ✢

Sandoval begins with the story of Andrés Dorantes. Rather than return to Spain where only the past awaits him, he accepts an offer to remain in Mexico City, taking up residence in one of the many royal hotels. Dorantes has decided to write the epic story of their epic journey, both for the edification of those who follow them and, he quietly hopes, to claim some eternal space for himself in the grand history of the Americas. It seems like a simple task, for who else has such a story to tell? He has been given a fine desk, a bottle of ink, an array of quills, sheets and sheets of paper, and, worst of all, bottomless time.

Almost immediately, he finds himself lost again, unable to capture the words, or the right sequence of words, or the right tone and style, that would allow him to guide a reader through the serpentine trails of the Floridian undergrowth while rivers of cold sweat ran under his steel breastplate or to recapture those hungry nights on the flat Texan coast when they nourished themselves on a thin stew of boiled crab shells. He starts over and over, throwing off the false words and distracting details that keep buzzing around his mind like a swarm of mosquitoes:

"Verily, the chief who presided over his people was of the most curious sort, even amidst this vast expanse of oddities. His peculiar nature was evident both within and without, for he loomed over his subjects, and elevated himself further by fashioning his matted locks into an elaborate crown of sorts, which was adorned with chicken bones and slender strips of deer hide. Nonetheless, it would be remiss not to acknowledge the dignity and grace that marked his bearing, as was befitted his station as a savage and noble lord."

Sometimes he even believes he is nearing the end before realizing that the story he's told is all wrong (wasn't that the chieftain of an entirely different tribe?) or lost down a false path (why linger so long on their accidental healing when it might not be read as a token of blessing but a mark of demonic arrogance?). Then he must go all the way back to the very beginning, when they first realized their ship was sinking, and try again, with better, more honest words.

How hard can it be, he asks himself, just to give everything its proper name and put it in its proper order? Isn't it like walking, one foot in front of the other, and eventually you get there? To add just the right detail, something vivid and a touch exotic, here and there so that a reader can hack his way through the thick, wet reeds while leaning back into the leather armchair that's been a fixture of his library for three generations now? Sometimes just to prove he knows his own story, Dorantes will mumble it aloud as he paces back and forth in his room, and he often practices in taverns as well, where he's become a well-known bore. But as soon as he sits down again, it's as though he's fallen into another fever, and everything becomes indistinct.

Years pass, a decade, a second. Dorantes is all but forgotten, and whatever words he continues to write and cross out and write again, to rephase and reorder, whatever pointless stories he first exaggerates beyond belief and then strips back down to a cool, empty core, only lead him further into a past that loops endlessly around itself and has no way out.

✢ ✢ ✢

Unlike his friend, Alonso del Castillo Maldonado seizes the opportunity to return to his home, securing passage on the next ship sailing across the Atlantic. He stays below deck as much as possible. At his estate outside of Salamanca, he is greeted with tears of joy by his loving family, who, despite all reason, had never doubted this day would come. In a room off the library, his wife shows him a shrine they had made many years ago, where they have prayed for his safety each morning and night. It is adorned with half-melted candles and the bric-a-brac of his past: his favored spoon, the bowl where he lathered his shaving soap, the elegant boots he wore on their wedding day.

His family had a portrait of Castillo painted in his absence, with his wife, two sisters, and aging father each advising the portraitist on his likeness, and the resulting work does bear a resemblance, but also looks cobbled together from their varied accounts, reflecting not a singular individual but some collective, unharmonious memory of one. He often sits in front of it and tries to recognize himself. He wonders why his family isn't more suspicious that he might be someone else entirely, an imposter in their midst. To him, that seems perfectly obvious.

"It's a miracle," his wife whispers to him one night, "a miracle that brought you back to me," and he feels a cold fear rush through him, because he also believes in miracles, but knows he is unworthy of any divine intervention. Ever since their fortunes changed on that long walk, he's never been quite sure what pact had been made and with Whom. While his estate feels like a little foretaste of heaven, especially in early fall when the grape harvest comes in, when he can hear children laughing through the shutters, he suspects this may just be the gentlest ring of hell, from which every path descends deeper.

One winter he begins to feel a strange ache in his shoulder, and when he pushes his fingers into the soft flesh connecting his arm and chest, he feels something hard, almost pointed and chiseled. Over several months it seems to grow, and then to sometimes twist and burn. Remembering that warrior, he wonders if he could trick someone into cutting it from him, but he knows this curse would only appear again in someone else, perhaps in one of his children or their cousins, perhaps his wife. So, he does nothing, nothing but wait, and as the pain eventually overwhelms him and he sinks, once again, into a fever, he finds himself in the Texan hills, stretched out on a woven mat with vultures circling above, with vultures scratching about him on the hard ground. When he lifts his head, he can see his friends and their entourage, joined by that horrible warrior, walking away from him. The only one who turns is Esteban, whose face is painted red and white.

✢ ✢ ✢

As for Cabeza de Vaca, he returns home to Cadiz, where he is reunited with his wife and family, who had first feared and then assumed his death. The governor had given him gifts, trinkets really, that he distributes among them, but most of what he's brought back are disturbing stories and a kind of restlessness that pushes everyone away. He can no longer sleep on a mattress and their rich food makes him sick. After a year trapped in their house, he journeys to Madrid to seek a royal audience. He appeals to those within the king's orbit to put him in charge of another expedition of discovery. Eventually his wish is granted. He is made governor of Paraguay, tasked with finding a pathway over the Andes to the rich mines of Peru.

After sailing back across the Atlantic, he begins another difficult journey, with its own set of disasters and miscalls, but somehow, even when the men inevitably begin to die and his army is crippled by fear and lethargy once again, it never feels like more than a pale reflection of that first adventure. It's as though he knows precisely what will happen next but cannot stop it. As though he knows precisely what words to say, but it will make no difference. His actions and speech lack all conviction. They are like echoes from another time that actually mattered.

Deep in the Amazon jungle, with the food running thin and his men insisting they turn back, he recognizes his moment. He has, after all, been here before.

It was then that a band of fierce warriors appeared from the jungle, and they beseeched the Spaniards to travel with them, for their chieftain had taken a grave turn, and they yearned for aid in his time of dire need. While his men prevaricated, insisting, surely, there was some easier way and questioning what duty they might owe to an idolator, Cabeza de Vaca recognized the moment and all the strange promise it offered. He told his men they, good Christians, could not refuse the call of duty, and so they set forth on yet another perilous journey, undeterred by the unknown dangers that lurked in these dense woods.

After several mosquito-plagued hours and swamp crossings, they could at least hear a rising din that betrayed the presence of a multitude, and the jungle parted. Cabeza de Vaca led his men into their village, where they were greeted by a throng of curious and awe-struck natives who had heard tell, no doubt, of the Spaniards potent medicines and arcane knowledges. In a finely constructed shelter at the center of the village, raised upon a dais piled high with deer skin and other pelts, their chieftain lay gravely ill, his body wracked with fever and shaking with chills.

Although his men urge against it, Cabeza offers to heal the chieftain. He prays, chants, and blows smoke deep into the poor man's lungs. He demands they build a greater fire. That they boil water from the river. That they bow their heads and listen to his prayer. He prays more loudly. But still the chieftain dies. Whatever magic he once had, whatever divine or infernal protection once watched over him, has left him behind. At that point his men, who never trusted Cabeza's easy ways with the natives, contrive to have him arrested, and from there they fight their way backward to the coast.

Eventually Cabeza de Vaca is returned to Spain in chains where he lives out his days, poor and forgotten.

✢ ✢ ✢

The final several hundred pages are devoted to Esteban, who had been abandoned by his friends as a gift to the governor. It's a betrayal, of course, but not the worst of them, because he has nowhere else to return to, and in Mexico he may be a possession, but he knows he is a prized possession. The governor and his aides interview him repeatedly. They show him the various maps they've tried to assemble, ask his assessment of possible paths. He responds with vague and tantalizing suggestions. He eats well and is cared for.

But life in the capital, for all its comforts, is still a cage of sorts, and he longs to get back into the wild. Or, at least beyond any Spanish domain. He suffered greatly along the trail, but he also wore turkey feathers in his hair, made strong men weep and women gasp. And he'd learned to heal the sick — even the dead, he sometimes suggests,

Colin Hamilton   117

knowing it both alarms and intrigues these Catholics. Accordingly, he starts to remember more and more, hints he'd heard along the way of gold and empires just a little further over the horizon, how a few clans seemed to recognize the Lord's Prayer. Before long the governor is obsessed with a new expedition to rescue those lost bishops and all their gold. It is to be led by Father Marcos, who will take Esteban as a guide with a small company of soldiers and native porters.

It's tough going, not just because the country is hard and dry and prickly, but also because Marcos and Esteban are immediately at odds, each pointing in a different direction. Whenever a little ribbon of smoke can be seen along the horizon, Esteban leans toward it while Marcos pulls away, and when they do cross paths with strangers, Esteban will spend the night joking, feasting, and dancing with the people they meet while Marcos sits solemnly apart in judgment.

The farther they pass from Mexico City, the clearer it becomes to Marcos how little control he has over his guide. God knows where he is being led. He tries to rally the soldiers to his side, whispering about Esteban's sinful behavior, about the way he leers at the native women and how they giggle sinfully in reply, but the soldiers are a less prudish sort, and some find themselves drawn to Esteban's mysterious and capable ways.

Weeks become months spent wandering through deserts and canyons. They find dusty villages and trickling creeks, but none of it suggesting any proximity to a land of wealth, and yet Esteban continues to insist they are getting closer. It is clear he is mistranslating the words of these locals, who are probably advising them to turn back, to give up. The two men argue every morning and night. Or Marcos argues and Esteban does whatever he pleases.

Then: At first Marcos assumes it is just over-exposure to the sun that blurs his vision and weakens his legs, but soon he recognizes that what's besieged him is a fever of some kind. For three days he lies shivering on the hot desert floor, in the shade of a rock, arguing with his angels. They want him to go home, to give up this fool's errand. But gold, he explains, for Spain and the king! I can't let that devil find it. He can see the fiend dancing naked with a crown of cactus thorns on his horrible head.

When he finally wakes and regains some lucidity, the men who have remained with him explain that Esteban has gone on ahead with several of the soldiers and most of the Indian porters. They have promised to mark their trail by leaving crosses along the path, and by the size of the crosses they will signal how close they have come to the Seven Cities. Marcos knows that it is madness to play along with Esteban's game, but they pack up what little food remains, what little water, and set off down the trail.

On the first day, they find a series of crosses — really just twigs dug into the dry dirt with broken stems balanced horizontally across — no higher than a man's knee, but toward the end of the second they discover one that reaches up to Marcos' waist. The land is just as barren, but they find themselves filled by an unexpected, unexplainable hope, and the crosses continue to creep higher. On the fourth day, one is even with Marcos' chest. When on the next they find nothing at all, a kind of despair passes among them, but not long after they spot another far off on the horizon — it must be the size of a man. All morning they walk toward it, and when they finally arrive, they can see it is all gnarled wood, some half burned by fire, a sickly thing.

It marks a trail that leads down into a deep, cathedral-like canyon layered with shades of red rock. They've never seen anything like it. When they call out for their companions, their own voices come echoing back. There is sand and stone, a breed of cactus that grows low to the ground with long, stiff needles. There are lizards pressed against the rocks in the sun. There are eagles circling above. At the end of the trail there is a small creek running with cool, clean water, which they camp beside.

The next day they scour the site, trying to find some marking, some direction that had been left for them, but it seems utterly bare. As the sun grows stronger, Marcos' eyes begin to ache and become less reliable, but at one point he is almost certain he can see another cross high up above them, there on an upper ridge of the canyon. As he tries to focus his gaze on it, to hold it, it suddenly moves, and what had been an extended arm rises up and waves slowly in his direction. It's just a man, he realizes, walking away from them.

And a satisfying last touch. Rather than ending there, with writer, reader, and Marcos all united in their fatigue, in their frustration with being bound to and led on a hopeless, pointless journey to nowhere by a trickster, Sandoval gives the final chapter back to his true hero. Esteban and the little tribe he's assembled, ex-soldiers and locals too, watch Marcos and his retinue pack their bags and head back the way they'd come. With that liberating absence, Esteban turns the other way, unbound and hopeful. The hills they're heading toward are all gold, at least in the blazing sun. He fingers the arrowhead he's carried with him as a charm.

THE AMERICAN WRITER WALTER MILLER JR. IMAGINED a post-nuclear, monastic library that collects and copies books of science and engineering, preserving knowledge until the world is ready to begin the entire process again, culminating in a second nuclear apocalypse.

✢ ✢ ✢

Where Angels Reign: A Record of My Voyage Through the Southern Seas with the Purported Scientist Charles Darwin

Hamish Mountolive

In 1258, Mongol armies sacked Baghdad, which held within its high walls an unparalleled collection of scrolls and parchments, reflecting both ancient wisdom and the most revolutionary new ideas. Shell-shocked contemporary historians tried to document the scale of human loss (perhaps two hundred thousand lives), but they saved their poetry for Baghdad's lost libraries, including the legendary House of Wisdom. Rather than reporting the Tigris ran red with blood, they mourned that it had been turned black by the ink of desecrated books. The fall of Baghdad and its libraries marked the beginning of the end of an Islamic Golden Age.

(History isn't circular, but it does make imperfect loops. Five hundred years earlier, at the Battle of Talas, the ascendant Ottoman Turks had defeated the Tang, whom many consider the high point of Chinese civilization and exemplars of cosmopolitan culture. It is believed that prisoners from this battle, taken to Muslim Samarkand, first introduced the secrets of papermaking to the West. Previously, parchment made from animal skins had been the principal source for codices, which meant that as many as two hundred fifty sheep may have been required to produce a thousand-page Bible. A precursor to the printing press, the introduction of paper fostered an early boom in written culture.)

Some have speculated that this terrifying, sudden reminder that everything a society had learned and protected over centuries could be lost so suddenly radically intensified the encyclopedic impulse —

that desire to condense, organize, and transmit knowledge in a form that could outride invading armies, even those mounted on Siberian ponies. A second theory, less evocative but perhaps more reliable, links the rise of encyclopedic work to the scale of knowledge having reached a point where no educated person could possibly be expected to have read everything, let alone remember it, thus creating the need for abridgments, summaries, abstracts, and other substitutes for the limitations of the human mind.

It was in this uncertain cultural moment, and about fifteen hundred miles to the west, that a former Egyptian bureaucrat elected to fill his retirement years by gathering all human knowledge and divine wisdom in a single compendium, which he, Shihab al-Din al-Nuwayri, appropriately titled *The Ultimate Ambition in the Arts of Erudition*. For its creation, al-Nuwayri worked in a study in Cairo, drawing upon older, frequently contradictory sources he had assembled through his wide travels on behalf of the Mamluk Empire, upon the various wise and experienced men he'd met, and upon his own considerable judgment. *The Ultimate Ambition* documents the many Bedouin words for the night sky ("the Encrusted, because of its abundance of stars, the Forehead, because of its smoothness . . ."), the nesting habits of flamingos, erotic poetry, the price of chickens and quince, the substance of clouds, the administrative details of promissory notes, and a survey of proposed treatments for impotence, among countless other explorations. It encompasses precise recipes and directions, as well as improbable folktales, such as a story about a lustful she-bear who takes a well-endowed man captive in her cave and licks his feet raw so he cannot escape her.

In its totality, *The Ultimate Ambition* runs on for more than two million words over nine thousand pages across thirty volumes. For centuries it remained an essential reference for scholars in the Islamic world, though often in piecemeal form given its unwieldy totality. Editions and extracts circulated in seventeenth-century Enlightenment circles in France and Holland.

About seven hundred years after al-Nuwayri and in a time when his work was all but forgotten, the architect Ivan Nemec faced internal exile in Soviet Czechoslovakia after he was discovered to be in possession of Daniel Defoe's *Robinson Crusoe*. Nemec was denied the right to travel. He was not allowed to work. His mere presence became a danger to friends. To spare them, he retreated into an ever smaller, ever more private world — a single unit on the fourth floor of a concrete housing complex in a sea of concrete housing projects so drab that parents would paint giant fruit on the sides of buildings so their children wouldn't get lost on their way home from school. He survived on surreptitious acts of kindness, seemingly random moments of bureaucratic reprieve, and by bartering away his possessions piece by piece.

With nothing else to do, and inspired by medieval mnemonic practices that he'd absorbed from one of his father's psychology manuals, he began to write something — a zoology of sorts, an encyclopedia not of "ultimate ambition" but an intensely personal nature. In total, he described the seventy-six objects that constituted the elements of his shrunken world, a thin collection that was later published, in samizdat, as *An Ark for One*. It includes:

The kitchen table is a circle divided in half, like a flat world with a single river. This is winter: the river is frozen; the wood is covered in ice and there is nothing to eat. Dust has collected inside the sun, which hangs from the sky by a cord. A long time ago, the moon rolled off the edge of the world.

The bathtub is too white: only a pearl diver would believe it, or the oyster herself. And smooth, as though that rough pearl had been passed from nervous child to nervous child to nurse. In a perfect world, where rivers are milk, all canyons would deepen like this. But the world isn't perfect, so the bathtub remains an animal: one tusk crusted by lime, a grated nostril, a chained rubber tongue.

The heater is caged in a long, tin box. When it is too cold to sleep and the heater wakes, it clatters against the mechanics of its cage, hissing through the grated top. Lumps of coal burn in its belly. Its hot breath blackens the wall.

While Nemec's self-contained, elegiac practice seems very different from the ravenous curiosity of al-Nuwayri, with one resigned to his lonely subjectivity and the other aspiring to enduring, foundational truths, at some level they are companion pieces: generated by men living in troubled times who understand their world through its pieces, whether those are modest and dwindling or nearly infinite. Both are driven by an aspiration to capture and preserve, to assemble and rearrange the elements of their world into some form or vessel that could be protected from the terrible forces of erasure.

I thought of both al-Nuwayri and Nemec when I happened upon *Where Angels Reign: A Record of My Voyage through the Southern Seas with the Purported Scientist Charles Darwin* by Hamish Mountolive, the expedition's junior surgeon, a narrative situated somewhere between those two mirrored extremes. Although rarely mentioned by Darwin, and then only dismissively ("the clumsy Liverpudlian," "a young man more lemur than ape"), Mountolive was part of the crew that helped determine the longitude of Rio de Janeiro, watched Argentine gauchos bola down ostriches, and discovered, at Punta Alta, a gigantic fossilized rhinoceros whose bones, Darwin wrote, "tell their story of former times with almost a living tongue." Mountolive met Jemmy Button, a shipwrecked sailor who had happily settled with natives at the far south of the world. On the Galapagos, he rode the giant, lumbering tortoises, and gazed into the eyes of the "imps of darkness," as they called the black marine iguanas. He watched, first with curiosity then growing discomfort, as Darwin noted the slight variations in the beaks of finches as they passed from rock to coast to isle.

It may be worth noting that rather than *The Stallion, The Lionhearted,* or *The Elizabeth,* the legendary ship that carried Charles Darwin to Tierra del Fuego, the Galapagos, and around the world was named for a small, noisy hunting dog. And that *The Beagle's* captain, the robustly christened Robert FitzRoy, almost declined Darwin passage because he felt that the shape of Darwin's nose prefigured a damning lack of determination, a concern that captured Victorian society's interest in the connection between physical traits and personal character, a flawed but perhaps inevitable step in our recognition of natural selection. Also, Darwin was known to tear thick books in half to make them easier to read.

While Darwin's discoveries would ultimately allow him to unearth a revolutionary truth, the crews' conversations and debates led Mountolive to a conclusion more in line with their times: "I've come increasingly to suspect that God assigned the holy task of creation to his most poetic angels, rather than those with a basic knowledge of engineering." (Some decades earlier: "If an angel were to tell us something of his philosophy, I believe many propositions would sound like 2 times 2 equals 13" — Georg Christoph Lichtenberg.) Pursuing this theme over the long and at times spectacularly dull five-year, round-the-world voyage, Mountolive, in the privacy of his journal, in the boredom of his nights, in the resentment of his neglect, gave himself license to become that angel himself and recount, in his angel voice, how our world came to be. Interrupting his long pseudoscientific observations are scores of asides that today read something more like prose poems, written from the perspective of an assistant deity or heavenly bookkeeper, there by God's side through his grand acts of creation.

A few of my favorites.

ON EVE. Her ripe flesh made snakes of us all. The whole garden was aslither. We offered her whatever fruits we could find: the Orange of Power, the Pear of Beauty, the Blueberry of Life. She chose the Apple of Knowledge. Why? Well, surely, she knows now, wise as she's become. As for myself, I suspect, ignorant as she was, the choice meant nothing to her then. Perhaps she liked the color red? Perhaps, as we waved the fruit before her, she glimpsed Adam beyond us with his simpleton's smile, scratching the peacock's throat? As her mouth closed around it, her eyes opened wide.

ON ENOUGH. *Some things we intended to keep only for ourselves. We always had our reason, and always a Prometheus who defied it. So too with Enough. You don't find it often among your humankind, who live like waves, willed on and on until the rough rocks break you to a fine, salty mist. Sometimes, though, a man passing from one town to another on his way somewhere else will stop. Sometimes turning the pages of his life, a boy will say, "This one." Then, it is as though his humanity has to go on without him. You can see it slipping away, expression by expression he'll no longer need.*

ON MIRRORS. *When one of my kind would travel among yours, we'd sometimes pass as merchants. This put you at ease. In crowded tents, at desert crossroads, we'd hoch our gaudy trinkets, the worthless waste of heaven: Gold, Bracelets, Fire and Hair. For such goods, you'd murder and weep. You'd bind our daughters' hands and show us their teeth. Sometimes we wanted more. You learned to bargain. To give up one soul, you asked for another in return. We showed you the Mirror. You framed it, like another god, in silver. You stared into its cold glass, watched its shallow eyes flicker, mimicked its every gesture.*

ON QUILLS. *I watched you walk through the tall, dry grass in the gray light of dawn, just as, on different days, I'd watched you lacing the sea with your nets, plucking petals from the rose. Why must you kill what you cannot become? A pheasant broke through the weeds, broke free of the weeds and rose, a mad flutter of wings. You aimed. The sky cracked. The pheasant fell. You'll say it was a test of skill, not malice. You'll say it feeds your child's hunger, not your own. But I saw you pluck a feather from its tail, test the hard quill against your thumb. And I could already read in that little book of yours the words, "I'm flying."*

ON GRASS. *A million pens struggling to dip themselves in the sky's blue inkwell. If they could ever reach, what would they scribble — of worm world, of the moles' dark coupling, of our mothers' new faces? Perhaps they'd call the grind of continental rocks God's Teeth? Perhaps what one blade whispers to the next is the epic history of grass, how it spread from field to field, conquering clovers. How once, long ago, its great, dead king learned to flower.*

ON SPIDER. *The fly, frenzied by the stink of waste, darts from rot to rot. Above him, spider dreams her web. Into the vacant vast surrounding, she casts a thought — some whispery notion made half real by the spinning of her gut. And somehow it catches a distant leaf, catches and in so doing begins to knot together this empty space. How many times have you stood, armed with a pen, helpless before a blank page? And how do* *you compare to this creation: crossing the nothingness on a thread of one's own self, bringing form to the formlessness of air? Slowly, her web is drawn, and who is to say there is a more perfect map of our cosmos, a better projection of one's secret soul? Imagine then the spider's trembling rage when the dung-drunk fly becomes entangled in her thoughts.*

THE ANGLO-IRISH WRITER JONATHAN SWIFT IMAGINED a library that was not a quiet, contemplative place, but one in which books representing the wisdom of the ancients do actual battle with books representing the wisdom of the moderns, leaving all the volumes torn, damaged, and diminished.

✜ ✜ ✜

A Mind of Winter
Antonia Wallace

Among Antonia Wallace's six largely unread books, perhaps the least appreciated and most unread — and surely the most *unjustly* unread — is *A Mind of Winter*, which imagines a future in which scientific leaps, anchored in gene editing, pharmaceutical precision, and surgical enhancement, have allowed humans to alter any number of physical imperfections and fragilities, thereby first escaping aging and ultimately the necessity of death itself, although it continues to linger, wolf-like, on the margins of society, occasionally making an unexpected, violent entry into this otherwise protected time.

In our era of dystopian obsession, a more predictable author might imagine a world in which everyone is granted permanent youth apocalyptically. It's not hard to project the angles: the exhaustion of natural resources that goes into sustaining endless life; the infinities of boredom that accumulate like barnacles on the years; the nihilistic thrill-seeking of the near immortal; the supremacist ideology that progressively narrows the gene pool to a single ideal of perfection. (I was just reading a review of a new book, Chana Porter's *The Seep*, in which an alien entity discreetly invades Earth, solving all of our problems and eliminating our humanity in the process...) The society Wallace describes, however, is mostly idyllic, and her future, by any historic standard, is a well-fed and tolerant place. But.

But despite all the promise of eternal youth and a generous diet of antidepressant-infused beef-like proteins, there are in Wallace's future still some who fall victim to "a mind of winter" and indulge an inner compulsion not just to give in to their own decline but also to embrace all that it means to age and weaken, to die. These people, "the rotters" as they are called, are deeply disturbing to their robust, beautiful peers, and are perceived as another virus in their midst to be expelled, a societal glitch, a flawed algorithm.

Most are shunned and driven away like lepers of another age, but Wallace's world retains our dual reaction to horror, both repulsion and, for some, an irrepressible compulsion to pull back the curtain. *To touch it.* Beneath the elegant, logical sheen of this world, a subculture has developed in which those who embrace their own ends become something akin to performance artists, enacting their decline in the far corners of the dark web or through secret cabarets for the entertainment of voyeurs.

(In an earlier book, warming to her theme, Wallace writes about a future in which the heavily drugged rich abandon sleep but miss their dreams. Scientists devise a device that allows them to exploit a vulnerable underclass, who are drugged as well but into a near permanent slumber, and whose subconscious adventures are consumed by the wealthy. Poor performers are unplugged, while the most exotic dreamers are traded at extravagant prices with deals negotiated through agents.)

Wallace's story is told through the experience of Justine, an accomplished physicist who, despite her evident vim and vigor, has lived far into her second century. Intrigued by the rumors she's heard and perhaps by some primordial stirring in her enhanced hippocampi, one night she ventures with a crowd of colleagues into one of the underground, velveteen clubs where the aging gather and the curious stray. There she sees Clea.

Generations of middle-aged men in both fiction and reality have found themselves unnerved by adolescent flowering, and the story of their humiliating, doomed pursuit is one we know well. Wallace inverts this tale: restored Justine is fixated by Clea's exotic pallor, by the unknown liver spots that, leopard-like, ascend her arms. Every description is written in a way that eroticizes Clea's mortality, while marking Justine's robust health as sterile, scentless, and numb.

"*A Mind of Winter,*" Wallace said in an interview I found buried deep online after nearly giving up my search,

"is my rejection of the cult of possibilities in favor of the hard church of difficult pleasures. I find the young exhausting, but even worse are midlevel, middle-aged executives wearing shorts and baseball caps or grown couples on dates at Disney movies. Homes in which 'young adult' fiction comprises the only dozen books, displayed beside staged family photos in matching polo shirts. I'm appalled by adults who are applauded for speaking the truth when all they've done is throw a tantrum. There was a time when we strove toward rites of passage, celebrated them, when we fought to be accepted as adults, but increasingly I feel as though an entire generation, maybe three, would reject all the thrilling vertigo of maturity for one long, sloppy suck at the teat. It's as though, given another bite of the apple, we've opted for Edenic ignorance instead."

For Justine's curiosity-seeking friends, the evening's entertainment is a daring and momentary distraction, and they quickly return to the cloistered lives they've been leading, but the image of Clea in all her doomed glory has somehow attached itself to Justine and begins to infect her. In her physics journals, Justine finds herself drawn to articles about orbital, optical and particle decay, bedrocks of twentieth century thinking that her own highly praised work has called into question for their defeatist assumptions. She covers whiteboards with complex mathematical equations, that are meant to bring her peace but do not. She visits a spa and has the last two weeks peeled from her skin and sucked from her pores, but that little taste of death has burrowed deep. Eventually she goes back.

What she discovers is that she is far from Clea's only suitor. In fact, there are varied, equally perfect rivals — a plasticine game show host, a senator known for his moralistic stance against reproduction, a captain recently returned from a long space voyage two years younger than when he'd left — but there is something in Justine's urgent need that matches Clea's own lack of time, and a surreptitious affair is sparked.

Justine is first drawn to all the unknown, forbidden secrets of Clea's flesh, which are described in long and longing paragraphs:

Was it a dream? Justine gently, and then less gently, caressed Clea's now bare shoulders, the bones and softly draped skin, with its fine roughness and spotting. A county of leather and salt. Her muscles had thinned, no longer fighting back against another's touch, but giving, always giving. The tenderness of it all, the fragility. And then, most unexpectedly, a surge of heat that beaded Clea's skin with moist sweat and lit a companion flame within her lover. As Clea slowly cooled, Justine could linger, for hours, combing her fingers through her gray hair, not some ethereal, silken nothingness, but a substance coarsened by life. Oh, and the rasping moan that even rose, when properly wooed, into a heavenly, enveloping cough...

But the more dangerous seduction is ultimately by Clea's mortal thinking: the vitality of doing almost anything for a final time, the rare power one amasses by being able to say, "no more." Although Justine repeatedly begs Clea to accept her protection, to allow Justine to give her life, it is her own attachment to health that unravels.

At this point, *A Mind of Winter* devolves, unfortunately, into a rather traditional, even male, perhaps colonial novel, in which Justine, as a representative of an advanced society, sets out to save the seemingly weaker, more vulnerable Other, who never emerges as a fully realized character in her own right, only to find herself ultimately corrupted by Clea's primitive ways. "Going native," as it were, Justine abandons the world as she knows it, and the final chapter devolves into a long, lecturing monologue, not unlike the quote above.

THE MALAYSIAN WRITER YANGSZE CHOO IMAGINED the Library of Heaven's Temple, hidden deep within Beijing's Forbidden City. It is lined with volumes of every shape and size, from all across the world, and rich with rare and ancient manuscripts. Lost secrets, hidden truths abound. The challenge is entry, for only a select few are allowed within. One must prove oneself worthy of knowing. But how?

✧ ✧ ✧

An Interruption

At its apex, the Library of Alexandria was the greatest of its time, amassing several hundred thousand or even a million scrolls gathered from Greece and the Eastern Mediterranean, Persia, and India. At first the collection grew through official requests to the counterparts of Ptolemy III, who were asked to lend prized manuscripts that his army of scribes would reproduce, but over time the Alexandrian authorities became more aggressive in their tactics, and when ships would enter the city's harbor, any scrolls they carried would be seized and taken away to be copied. Once complete, the Alexandrians would return the duplicate to the ship while the original was preserved within their library.

To put the library's scale in perspective, when Gutenberg developed his press *seventeen hundred years later,* there probably weren't even fifty thousand books, the technology that replaced scrolls, in all of Christian Europe, and the majority were copies of the same handful of religious texts. The Muslim world was, thankfully, far richer in its archives. Over the fifty years that followed Gutenberg, printing presses would produce somewhere between eight and twenty million physical, individual books on a continent that housed seventy to eighty million people, and the range of titles began to widen in scope as well, increasingly embracing literature, philosophy, science, and history.

Fast-forward a few more centuries and hop across the ocean. To date, more than forty million *unique book titles* have been registered in the United States, and it is estimated that about three million new books (titles, not copies) are published each year, the majority self-published. Total annual book sales are approaching eight hundred million; a huge number moderated by this hard reality: most titles sell fewer than three hundred copies.

Meanwhile, the internet contains nearly two *billion* distinct websites and is adding three hundred million more while doubling in data-size every year with written words increasingly replaced by photos, videos, and streaming audio. Our Alexa is, appropriately, named in the library's memory.

But back to our story.

As the book lust of the Alexandrians became widely known, and as court officials of the Ptolemies were sent far and wide to harvest every scroll in all the written languages of the civilized world, it spurred a sub-industry of forgeries and fakes that could be sold for outrageous prices to acquiring agents, so that the quest for knowledge became entangled with deception and lies. The collection expanded, but in many cases, it would take centuries for scholars to sort out what was real and what was counterfeit, and in between competing, sometimes contradictory, versions of the same text sparked fierce debates and heresy.

Given this voracious, acquiring hunger, in time the Library of Alexandria became so vast that it was virtually unusable. The exhaustive became the exhausting. Nothing could be found readily within its many chambers, and as much was lost within it as remained beyond the city's reach. As a result, Callimachus of Cyrene, a patron saint of librarians, was appointed to bring order to chaos through a bibliographic survey of the library's collection that itself ran one hundred twenty volumes long, and which reminds me of the card catalogs of my youth that in some grand libraries filled entire rooms with rows of elegant oak cabinets and carefully typed and alphabetized index cards, some amended with notes scribbled in pencil.

It is easy to dismiss the library's growth as just another story of tyrannical avarice, replicated in vast tombs and unending walls, in ungovernable colonies and labyrinthine harems, but it is a mistake to reduce the desire to know to the desire to have. This was no dragon asleep on a bed of gold. Alexandria became a hub for thinkers who could measure the circumference of the Earth and mine the depths of Pi, and they helped to codify a classical canon that remained the foundation of intellectual life in Europe and Islamic North Africa and the Middle East for most of a millennium, even as societies collapsed and plagues raged, a dim spark of light in a dark time looking more and more like our own.

By the time of its disappearance, the Library of Alexandria was not a single building but a network of them, and it had been in decline for centuries as Rome and Constantinople lured the ambitious farther north and east. The *coup de grace* may have come in the seventh century, following an invasion by Caliph Omar and his army, who are said to have burned what remained of the library's scrolls to heat the city's bathhouses, although this romantic, or chauvinistic, legend papers over a more likely story of slow decay and abandonment, as well as the violent purges of Christian zealots that predated Omar by more than a century. Along with the library itself, we lost an almost unfathomable wealth of classical works, including the majority of plays by Aeschylus, Euripides and Sophocles.

✧ ✧ ✧

I've spent nearly half my life working in libraries, I've often found myself reflecting on this past, sometimes enthralled by its grandiosity when I'm on our upper floors and at other times, up to my knees in discarded books, shaking my head at the predictability of its end. Our library emerged out of a similar spirit, though more than two thousand years later: a provincial town that wanted to define itself not just by the lumber it produced, not just by the milled grains it sent down river, but as a place of sophistication, culture, and invention, of literacy and legitimacy. And it largely worked. Over a mere century we became a hub of product design and biomedical devices, renowned for our theaters and museums. Our library is both a source of continual rebirth and civic pride.

I've come across countless references to the Library of Alexandria in materials that span virtually every department in our own vast collection — history and fiction, of course, but also law, religion, music, agriculture, philosophy and medicine. More recently, however, I came across, in an article that led to another article that led to a single book, aptly titled *Sacred Trash,* reference to a different endeavor that mirrors of the work of the Alexandrians but in a warped, funhouse way, just as my own little library of discards reflects both what our library has rejected and what it rests upon.

In the centuries that followed Caliph Omar, Egypt, along with virtually all the lands bending south of the Mediterranean from Persia through Spain became a Muslim domain, although pockets of Jewish and Christian life continued to thrive, especially in complex communities like Cairo. There, just a couple hundred miles south and west of Alexandria, in the Ben Ezra Synagogue, which is said to have been built on the site where the baby Moses was once discovered among the weeds, something unremarkable in the moment happened. Someone, perhaps a rabbi or another elder of congregation, knocked a hole in an inner wall, creating an access point to a small interior clearing protected from sun and rain, and he used this space to deposit written material that could was no longer wanted but which could not simply be thrown away. This service was so useful, necessarily even, to the Jewish community of Cairo that for centuries that followed people filled this hidden room with books and other documents written in Hebrew, Arabic, and Aramaic, as well as other languages common to the times, on vellum, paper, papyrus, and cloth.

Versions of this sanctuary, called a genizah, were found in many early and medieval Jewish communities, where there was an outright ban on throwing away any material that might include the name of God or any scriptural passage or reference, which in practice could include a vast array of documents both religious and secular. And yet, the practical challenges of these communities were no different from our own — storage, the crushing weigh of the irrelevant, and a simple need to clear a path. Genizahs were designated areas where written materials could be discarded prior to a formal burial of written words, which was meant to occur every seven years, but in some cases, like in Cairo, the genizah would amass documents over decades or even centuries. While written material in a genizah could not be thrown away, it was allowed — like a body — to disintegrate. Even today, many synagogues collect worn religious books for proper burial, and in Jerusalem, perhaps elsewhere, temporary genizah — essentially recycling bins like we might more commonly see for used clothing — can be found on the streets.

In an abstract form, a genizah, which is commonly translated as "hidden" or "concealed," was intended for two primary forms of materials, those of either a sacred or profane character. Sacred materials needed to be protected and honored, even after they were no longer required, whereas subversive materials needed to be quarantined. But over time many genizah, and especially the Cairo Genizah, became a storage space for any obsolete document. Its contents include personal letters, legal contracts, writs of divorce, money orders, magic charms, and countless other ephemera, as if eventually the sacred, profane, and mundane all become distinguishable. Which most of us, in our own lives, know to be true.

Making sense of the material in the Cairo Genizah has been compared to reassembling hundreds of comingled jigsaw puzzles that have been allowed to rot and decompose for centuries, but out of these pieces archivists have assembled an entirely richer understanding of Jewish life in Eastern Mediterranean in the Middle Ages — what people wore and complained about, where they traveled, how they intermingled with their Christian and Muslim neighbors, the spells they cast to enhance their erotic conquests (a practice that, not surprisingly, involved wearing your pants on your head while issuing a particular chant). The Cairo Genizah has also brought back to life some of this lost community's individuals, people like Abraham Ben Yiju, a Tunisian-born merchant who, more than one hundred years before Marco Polo, traveled to the Indian port of Mangalore, where he freed and married a local slave while establishing a business exporting cardamom, nuts, pepper, locks, and brass bowls to his partners in Aden. He spent eighteen years abroad, so many in fact, that when he could physically return, he struggled to rejoin his family and the Jewish community he'd left. Perhaps Ben Yiju led an extraordinary life, or perhaps not: who knows how many similar stories of dislocation and reinvention, of basic commerce exoticized by foreign products are scattered about in torn and decaying fragments, stuffed between the walls and left to molder?

Among the other finds, an original copy of an extremely rare and valuable second century B.C. book of wisdom, the proverbs of Ben Sira, which include this gem: "Hidden wisdom and concealed treasure. Of what value is either?" I liked that enough to tape it to the door of the discard room, and I was pleasantly surprised to see it still there when I returned the next day.

THE ENGLISH WRITER CHINA MIÉVILLE IMAGINED a Library of the Nameless, comprised of a vast collection of dangerous and forbidden books, some bound in human skin, some cursed, some sentient. Were they to fall into the wrong hands, their occult knowledge might destroy the world. Or just possibly enlighten it. Thus, the library is hidden away and guarded by a team of formidable librarians every bit as strange and threatening as the books they shelter.

✢ ✢ ✢

Fodder
Komas Dalaho

Fodder is a splinter, of sorts, of *The Iliad's* fifth book, one of the bloodiest in a bloody work.

Angered by Agamemnon's latest insult, Achilles refuses to rejoin the fight, and suddenly the emboldened Trojans are crashing down upon the Greek encampment. In these verses, Homer describes the deaths of twenty-seven Trojans and twelve Greeks. Rarely at a loss for graphic details, he gives us spearheads, lances, and heavy swords crashing through shoulders, ribs, skulls, neck cords, jaws, nipples, and tongues. Overwhelmed by their bloodlust, the gods, who've been banished to the sidelines by Zeus, can't restrain themselves any longer and rush into the fray. A frenzied Athena goads the Greek hero Diomedes into attacking her brother, Apollo. With Athena driving his chariot and screaming in his ear, he rams his heavy spear beneath Ares' breastplate and deep into his belly. Howling and outraged, the war god flees the battlefield. As Book Five ends, the field is scattered with bodies. And then Homer moves on.

Komas Dalaho — a Turkish Kurd whose parents fled Erdogan's repressive regime and raised their teenager in a North African enclave of Barcelona that became increasingly divided between its largely secular and militantly Islamic residents, leaving countless others caught in between — does not. In each of *Fodder's* twenty-seven stories, Dalaho memorializes Book Five's easily forgotten Trojan dead — mostly young, inconsequential boys.

Take, for example, Amphius, to whom Homer spared ten lines, the last of which involves Ajax stripping his corpse of its armor. From

Dalaho, we learn how Amphius came of age during the long years of the Trojan War, in the provincial land of Paesus, "rich in possessions, rich in rolling wheatland..."

The men of Paesus are mostly absent, sucked into doomed service to their overlords in Troy, except for the few who've returned with missing limbs and no war booty. At young ages the boys inherit the hard work of shepherding goats and plowing fields, work they do poorly, and each year their poor village becomes even more marginal and mean. The boys throw rocks and longing looks at the village girls. They plot raids on the next village over, but nothing comes of their chatter. Occasionally a traveling merchant or refugee, a crippled war veteran on a long journey home, will pass through, bringing news of their fathers and older cousins, a few of whom have done some transient, notable deed while others have died in service or simply disappeared.

One day it is a charismatic priest who appears in Paesus. After milling about for a bit and making himself known, he mounts a dusty stone in what passes as the village square and in a loud voice calls everyone to gather around him. It is an order that mostly goes ignored, except by a few with nothing better to do, although even those who pretend to continue on with their business and refuse to directly acknowledge him slow their work and allow his words to reach them. The boredom of their days is crushing.

He begins hesitantly, speculating about the health of their crops and sympathizing with their hardships, but as he rallies to his true theme, a kind of urgency weaves into his words. He proclaims that the gods are appalled by the arrogant Greeks, how they've disgraced Trojan homelands, humiliated the Trojan people, violated Trojan women:

*"But even worse, brothers and sisters, the gods are appalled by
we Trojans. For in the end, it isn't the Greeks who debased us
but we ourselves! And not just the royal house in the great city,
but all of us who serve them here in the hinterlands, for we have
allowed their sacred lands to be salted, their temples overturned.*

*"People of Paesus, are you not ashamed? You are. I can see it.
In fact, I believe shame is the only crop here that prospers, for it
is the only one you tend to day and night. Do you think it will
feed you come winter? You'd do better to suck on the cold teat of
death. Let that soothe your nerves.*

*"But there is, in all this shame and misery, there is still a
glimmer of hope. The gods have turned away because they can't
bear to look at what you've become, but hear me: pull back their
gaze! Rise up! Be worthy of their fierceness."*

Arming themselves with brooms and sticks, a council of elderly women chase him away, but not before his words — honor, revenge, eternal glory — can infect some of the boys. Outside of town, the priest sets up a camp that is sometimes visited by the thin-wristed adolescents. And there, beyond the reach of the tired elders, he tells these boys the stories of the great war that is raging not far over these hills, of the valiant, of destiny. So, they learn the names of those who have done immortal deeds, men who were once boys like themselves but dared to become something more.

While some quickly tire of the firebrand, others, including

Amphius, are mesmerized by his visions and drawn deeper into his scheming. At his bidding, one of these boys kills a prized goat, which they roast together under the stars; another steals and breaks an elder's staff. They report to their priest on the comings and goings of a young village woman whose man has gone to war, who's been away now for years, when and where the stranger might see her bathe. They bring him fresh bread and oil. He repays their sacrifices with stories of this war and its heroes they've never seen but who tower over their world and imaginations.

He tells the boys about the war's beginning, lingering on the cowardice of the famous Greeks. How Odysseus sought to avoid the struggle altogether, terrified that if he ever left his home it would take him years and years to return to its plump olives and his plump wife, so he feigned madness when the princes came to retrieve him, but they outsmarted him, the clever one, by placing his infant son in the path of an oxen plow; that, at last, awoke his manhood, and he sprang to his senses, rescuing the boy but dooming himself to servitude. How Achilles' mother dressed him like a girl so he'd somehow be overlooked by the recruiters, but, like the vicious killer he already was, he couldn't resist playing with their swords and spears. They stripped off his dress, hustled him aboard their ship, and left his mother weeping on the dock.

In some form or another, they already know these stories, and yet when the priest tells them once again, the village boys are drawn into his spell.

Although the war is only in its seventh year, the priest also tells them about its conclusion, which is beginning to approach.

After finally recognizing they will never breach Troy's mighty walls, the Greeks resort to their one true strength: deceit. They build an enormous wooden horse and fill its hollowed belly with their best men. Lesser men wheel it before the Trojan gates as an offering of peace before retreating back to their ships and sailing away. And at first the Trojans are deceived. With thick ropes, they drag the horse into their city square. They walk about it, reminiscing about the great battles and their dead brothers, and acknowledging that if nothing else, the Greeks are elegant craftsmen. This wooden horse is a marvel. Then they begin to celebrate, drinking wine and singing songs, and chasing women and girls, some of whom allow themselves to be caught.

But they've not all been debased, and one young warrior remains on guard. As he continues to inspect the horse, he thinks he can hear something stirring inside it, a whisper, a brush of metal against metal. Coming closer, he swears he can smell not just cedar but also something foul and sweating. On its underside, he detects a secret hatch and just before the devious Greeks can spring it open, he wedges the tip of his spear between the hinged boards. Now the Greeks are pounding against the door, rattling their swords and shouting their foreign words, and this warrior is summoning whatever strength he has to edge his spear tip deeper into the gap, sealing it shut, while screaming at the top of his lungs to summon the night guard, who manage to raise themselves.

Finally recognizing the danger, they hold their torches to the horse's belly until the whole beast and its secret army are set ablaze. Seeing the flames over the wall, the rest of the Greeks, who had secretly returned in the night, think the city has been taken and reveal themselves. Expecting the gates to be opened by their comrades, they are stunned when instead the Trojan army comes rushing out, chasing the Greeks back to the beaches and killing them off in the crashing surf.

"Can you imagine," the stranger asks, "being stuck here, in this meaningless village, on that beautiful night?"

All the boys love the story, but Amphius in particular, against his mother's wishes, finds himself drawn to this magnetic stranger, who speaks to him, at times, the way a father might, or an older brother. They increasingly ignore the goats, spending their days instead battling one another with wooden sticks, spying on the girls as they cool their feet in the stream. When the women try to talk some sense into them, they berate their elders.

Then one early morning, while the others sleep, the priest wakes Amphius and leads him out into a grove just over a rise from the village. He wants to share with him a strange dream he'd had in which Aphrodite had spoken to him directly.

"Do you know what she said," the priest asks. "That she favors you, Amphius. That she is waiting for you at Troy and has taken the form of a young princess in the house of Priam, one that Helen fears. That already she is laying a trap cleverer than Odysseus himself, planting before him an elusive string of images that assemble through his day — a pregnant mare pacing in the ring, red ants streaming from their nest, a simple latch that holds his serving girl's tunic closed, little sparks of burning ash that don't fall to the ground but rise up in the air.

Before long, he'll put the pieces together. And this is what she told me: that she needs you to be there when the horse arrives, to save your people from it. Are you ready to take up a spear and become a man? To avenge your village and become the savior of Troy? To be swept up in a god's lithe arms?"

We don't need Dalaho to tell us the boy's answer; Homer has already told the end of his story:

But destiny guided Amphius on, a comrade sworn
to the cause of Priam and all Priam's sons.
Now giant Ajax speared him through the belt,
deep in the guts the long, shadowy shaft stuck
and down he fell ...

I called *Fodder* a splinter, and that feels right to me. There is a thinness to it, but it is that very thinness that lets under your skin, a little irritant that slowly swells, that begins to ache. Across the other chapters, names change and motivations deviate, but the basic plot repeats ad nauseum, and always with the same end: another young boy heading off to war, with the reader knowing it will be a short and brutal one for him, generating nothing more than a passing phrase in some song and denied any grand adventure home.

THE AUSTRALIAN WRITER GERARD MURNANE IMAGINED out on the inner plains a library of inverted maps in which those places that are best known are rendered mysterious with mermaids, impossible beasts, and totemic symbols, while the far, untraveled lands are described in precise details, their streams and cities, railways, and banks.

✢ ✢ ✢

The Frivilous Ones
Ichiro Takamine (trans. Elena Uno)

Although virtually forgotten today, and when remembered at all, remembered with a kind of embarrassment, Ichiro Takamine was either blessed or cursed by early fame and, for a brief moment, considered a novelist of consequence. When his first book, *The Frivolous Ones,* was published in 1936, its portrayal of America — a country still largely unknown to the Japanese and shrouded in myth — struck a nerve with a generation of young men who'd been raised within one of the world's most adamantly isolationist nations, and for a time stories abounded of readers who abandoned their families and education, their pregnant young wives, to hop ship, cross the Pacific, and hit the Occidental road. Takamine was among the first modern Japanese authors to be translated into English and German, and when the French edition of *The Frivolous Ones* was released, André Gide, that generous champion of poorly aging books, declared it "an authentic masterpiece." "Brilliant," Thomas Mann echoed. I agree.

In the English-language edition I discovered, the title is boldly displayed in a hyper stylized font I can only imagine some American designer thought represented a Japanese notion of Americana. Spread across two of the opening pages is a hand-drawn map of the United States, with the various waters — the Pacific, the Gulf and the Atlantic, the Great Lakes, the Mississippi — inked a deep black and with a triple pen-line delineating their borders. A few cities, some famous and others virtually unknown, and landmarks (the Alamo, headwaters of the Mississippi, Old Faithful, the Appalachian Trail) are named, but long stretches are left blank. Presumably they don't matter to this tale.

Takamine's story begins just a little south of San Francisco in the early years of the Great Depression.

That night I slept in a ruined farmhouse, my only company, I hope, an owl who perched in the rafters, his wise head rotating back and forth, trying to find the right gaze to take me in, but I know I continued to elude him. Eventually he flew off for easier prey. In the morning I began to meander southward, not by any great intention, it just seemed like the right way to fall through this land, and my way took me through a long valley buffered by rolling hills. The days were hot, and I took to resting in ditches and groves, and I walked through the night to keep myself warm. Once I saw in the distance a little town and I could imagine myself pausing there for a few days or maybe a lifetime, but I felt myself turn away from it. Later I met a shallow-cheeked man walking as I was, who said I'd make the right choice to keep going. "They aren't good people," he said, "but a little further on this way and you'll find a farm where they're known to need an extra hand." As we were headed the same direction, we walked together talking about the stars, death, the relentlessness of change, honor among thieves, and love as well. Then he pointed me down a different path and our ways diverged.

The farm is a kind of paradise, fragrant and warm. As he begins to stir with the dawn, a crew of field hands, Okies, arrive in the backs of overloaded trucks. He's anxious that he'll be chased out of this Eden, but when the men discover him, they are kind and curious. Together they share a glorious, thick-skinned fruit and talk as best they can. Although his English is decent, their regional accents confuse him. They tell him about the Dust Bowl, describing tremendous grit-filled winds and waterless storms. When their crops failed, when their sinewy goats died and there was nothing left to feed their children, they were forced to abandon their homes and wander west, which is how they landed here, in California, although the story seems so incongruous with this abundant garden, he's not sure he really understands it. They'll never go back, they tell him, and advise him against going any farther himself. Maybe, they suggest, they could help him find work? But he goes on.

From there, *The Frivolous Ones* rolls out in a long, circuitous journey that is pushed along for reasons either unclear or so simple — to see the unknown, to be on the road — that they are never directly expressed. Our wanderer has almost no money and then loses what little he has, which puts him at the mercy of a carnival of characters he meets along the way, Americans mostly but also other Asians who for various reasons are also crossing the continent from west to east, against the grain of Manifest Destiny, and whose paths overlap in unexpected ways, in unexpected places. For example, a charismatic Indian doctor who issues a cryptic warning in Fresno reappears two hundred pages later at a roulette table on a Kansas City riverboat casino, where, after a lucky roll of the die, he refills our hero's pockets. The narrator tells many of the people he meets that he has an uncle in New York, a stockbroker, that most American of careers, who may be able to offer him a job if our hero can only make it there.

Arrested hopping trains, he spends a month in prison in Carson City, where he shares a cell with a taciturn Texan cowboy and a gregarious hobo who has abandoned the coal mines of West Virginia. A sympathetic guard masterminds their escape. He works, briefly, at a ranch in Wyoming. There he spends a hallucinatory night wandering the rings of a traveling circus, complete with a strong man, a contortionist, an impresario, and a fortune teller. In the northern woods, in the town of Sleepy Eye, Minnesota, he is taken in by a Norwegian immigrant farming family, whose daughter tries to seduce him into staying, although it is possible he simply misunderstands her strange manners.

While the narrator of *The Frivolous Ones* tells us very little about himself directly, we hear from others that he is "handsome," a term Takamine must put on the tongues of a dozen different women spanning generations and classes. He is also, we are told, young, emotionally remote, naïve, deceptive, heartless, arrogant; he is repeatedly mistaken for Chinese. In St. Louis, he visits enormous slaughterhouses, whose stench of death trails him for miles down the road. In New Orleans, he sleeps in the alleys of Tremé after the jazz bands finally shut down. That's where he's found by his former prison mate (the hobo, not the Texan), who buys him breakfast and shares a long story about his broken heart.

> *"If only you could have seen her, you'd understand me then and not think me such a fool! A painted and buxom thing, and tigerish too. Pure, yearning evil of the most delightful sort! She smelled of roses, bourbon, and turpentine, I tell you. I can still*

smell her now. She burns in my throat. Her husband, of course, was a brute, and what else could he have been, but I'll never forget that he'd saved me from a hanging party in Durango. Forgive me, no, she was a butterfly," and he began to flutter about as he spoke . . .

One of Takamine's most pronounced stylistic tics is a habit of describing people twice, often in diametrical terms. Sometimes the differences are physical, so that a woman with chestnut hair is, in the next paragraph, raven-like; her blue eyes turn, with a page, to gray. The tigerish become butterflies. But more frequently the instabilities are in character: a gentleman who initially exhibits an air of nobility is soon described by the crude shape of his mouth, the vulgar glint of his eye; a doctor who is introduced as thoughtful and wise is seen again, after a mere turn of his head, to be calculating. Often there is no explanation or even acknowledgment of these shifts, as if there were no reason at all to assume someone would remain the same from moment to moment. The second perception is almost always more threatening or uncomfortable than the first. I could never quite tell if this was meant to be a literary device, a worldview, or a dig at the American character.

While *The Frivolous Ones* is essentially a travelogue, Takamine isn't particularly interested in the road or the passages between here and there, focusing instead on points of arrival, the necessity of departure. Virtually every time he moves on, it is as an escapee; everyone he meets, it would seem, wants to hold him back. Each new episode begins with minimal transition or buildup, and we are taken aback to suddenly find our hero the guest on a Mississippi plantation, having seen him last hitching a ride out of the Crescent City. The patriarch, who could easily have been, and a few well-read critics insist *was*, lifted from a Faulkner novel, welcomes this new guest, though it's not clear he could leave if he wished. Not matching any of the existing castes, the narrator moves between the Jewish property manager, the Black farmhands, poor Whites, and the patriarch's inbred clan. Some nights, he's a Scheherazade, expected to entertain his host with stories of the exotic east, while on others he's subjected to the patriarch's long rants of decline and fall (more Faulkner).

In a moment that confuses both the narrator and the reader, he and the Jew are accused of some kind of deception; forewarned, they slip out in the middle of the night. In Charleston, he attends a Confederate-themed bacchanal. When he confesses how broken he's become, how far he's drifted from whatever it was that once made him real, a masked woman (who may be the circus fortune teller from Wyoming?) assures him, "It's not the urn but the shard that survives." Ultimately, he arrives in New York and the novel ends at the door of his uncle's office, which may be abandoned.

About a year after the book's original release, in the heat of its fevered acceptance, a reviewer revealed that Takamine, like Gide himself, and in fact like almost all of the book's most passionate admirers, had never actually set foot in America. Instead, he'd written it while immersed in an atlas and a series of travel guides and magazines — *My Time Among the Iowans, Life, Father Louis Hennepin's Description of Louisiana, The Journals of Lewis and Clark* — while drawing upon his love of American fiction — Melville,

Twain, Zane Grey, young Hemingway, young Faulkner, and most certainly Whitman too.

All this created a minor (literary, after all) scandal, but also a deep sense of betrayal among many of Takamine's readers, and especially among those who had become his acolytes or had even gone so far as to take up the mantle of restless wanderer. The next wave of reviews was far more likely to dismiss *The Frivolous Ones* as a compendium of stereotypes and superficial portraits. For a smaller circle, which became smaller and smaller over time, the revelation was instead a confirmation of Takamine's artistry.

As for Takamine, he seemed to take the criticism as a challenge. In each of his later books he defiantly wrote about people, places, and times that he himself had experienced only through the filters of literature and nonfiction, abandoning not just Japan but Japanese characters as well. In *The Fourteen Who Fled,* for example, Constantinople, which has stood for over a thousand years as the capital of the Eastern Roman Empire, has finally been overrun by the army of the twenty-one-year-old Mehmed the Conqueror. As the Ottomans swarm through the streets, those who can take what they can and flee, with some resurfacing in Greek colonies across Thessaly and Italy, others into Greater Bulgaria and Moscow, Syria, and Spain. Each of the chapters follows one of those who fled and, more critically, how something they carried — the Justinian Code, the geometrical theorems of Archimedes describing the area of a circle and the volume of a sphere, the expression of religious devotion in a curved mosaic, a certain shade of blue — takes root in some new world and flowers. It was poorly received.

Unbowed, Takamine insisted that he'd never leave Japan, and then that he'd never leave his native city of Kyoto, and then that he'd never leave the small district where he lived. He spent his final years as a recluse in a small home with its enclosed garden, writing a series of genre novels — *The Riders Code, Under Thunder Rock, East of Hope* — about Chilean Patagonia and an outfit of heroic, misfit gauchos battling against an influx of robber baron ranchers.

THE AUSTRALIAN ANTHROPOLOGIST THEODORE STREHLOW DID NOT SO MUCH IMAGINE as attempt to document a complexly structured oral or "song library," through which a nonwritten culture, the Arrernte, could nevertheless archive its beliefs, cosmographies, history, and terrain, a particularly difficult, and perhaps inherently misguided, task as illustrated by the betrayal so many Arrernte felt when the British writer and wanderer Bruce Chatwin became the primary interpreter of their songs.

✢ ✢ ✢

A Guide to Universal Grasping
Nathan Park

"What *Ulysses* is to the novel, what 'The Waste Land' is to twentieth-century poetry, what *The Road to Oxiana* is to travel writing, so is *A Guide to Universal Grasping* to technical manuals."

These words, attributed to Jack McFarland, CEO of Dyonysis Robotics, are quoted in the pitch copy on the back cover. I confess they left me both intimidated — for I know how limited my capacity to read any technical manual is, even a simple guide to my toaster, let alone one that draws comparison to great and notoriously difficult literature — and also intrigued. Was it a joke? And if not, what could it possibly mean? It would be something of a lie to say I loved *Ulysses* or "The Waste Land," or that I'd ever reached the end of *The Road to Oxiana* (presumably Oxiana itself), but as identifiers, they lit up blinking neurons somewhere deep in my skull, beacon signals that lured me toward a kind of destiny I thought of as my own. As I rotated the book, I came back to its front cover, which bears a complex industrial illustration of something vaguely hand-like, fingered with an assortment of digits and tools, not unlike a surreal Swiss army knife, rotating through three-dimensional space and seeming to move toward the reader with programmed intent.

I tried to leap in midstream, opening Park's book to a random page, but found the copy nearly impenetrable, and so I circled back to the start, an introduction by McFarland added to the second edition. From that I learned "universal grasping" is a kind of holy grail in the field of logistical robotics. It describes a machine that is not designed for, and thus limited to, a single task or range of functions, but able to orient itself to and clutch any object it is assigned to retrieve — loosely packed ping-pong balls, a refrigerator, a goldfish in a soft pouch of water, a finely tuned medical device, a single sheet of paper — before moving it to a desired location. Such a robot would radically transform modern warehouses, where human agility and adaptability continue to outmaneuver our would-be AI overlords, much to the frustration of payroll departments. Park's magnum opus is, as described by McFarland, an analysis of various failed attempts to achieve this ultimate adaptability and an extended speculation about alternative design solutions that may point inventors toward a future of increased human irrelevance and corporate efficiency. Reminiscent of obsequious medieval texts written to the king, Park's manual is dedicated, hopefully, to Jeff Bezos.

A Guide to Universal Grasping is not a book to be read standing up, so I saved it for an afternoon coffee break when I hoped an infusion of caffeine would make my mind clearer and more focused. With an emptied mug beside me and the comfortable buzz of others making a kind of white noise machine, I worked my way through the first few pages with what I would quickly recognize as a false sense of confidence. Before long I could hardly say that what I was doing was *reading*, though it might appear that way to an observer. My eyes scanned across Park's impenetrable sentences:

> *... a unified model is introduced to evaluate the productivity and ergonomic performance of collaborative robotic systems with time used to represent strain index and per unit of work effort time, while a cylinder head assembly is introduced for*

asynchronous applicability under mechanized dimensions, which we adopted two- and three-dimensional polynomial functions to detect CP and represent simple fitting models obtained by solving the following simultaneous linear equations...

These are then frequently interrupted by complex mathematical equations in which symbols and letters have replaced numbers:

$$F_h = \frac{\mu \Delta x_l p d \pi d_c \cos \gamma}{2\pi d + 8l_0 - 4L_0} + \frac{\mu p \pi d h_c (d_c - d_n)}{d - d_n}$$

And:

$$\sum F_{y2} = 0 \Rightarrow \int_0^\Pi p \sin \varphi \frac{d}{4} dw_l d\varphi - 2T_l = 0 \Rightarrow T_l = \frac{pd}{8} dw_l$$

By the time I gratefully reached a period, I had virtually no sense of what had been said or how the grammatical components fit together into some structural whole. As a compromise, I found myself underlining paired words and short phrases, as though they might offer essential clues that I could later, in some mythical time when I'd learned the foundations of mechanical engineering, reassemble into meaning:

...adversarial objects...
...failure of the policy...
...parameters governing physics...

... imprecise actuation and calibration ...

... inherent uncertainty in sensing, control and contact ...

... heterogeneous grippers ...

... parallel-jaw and vacuum-based suction ...

... per-object reliability ...

... domain randomization ...

... a memory system that avoids repeated mistakes ...

... binary rewards ...

... algorithmic supervisor ...

... catastrophic forgetting can lead to unpredictable failures ...

... arbitrary constellations of objects ...

... logic not explicitly programmed but emerging from synthetic training ...

... bloodworm inspired gripper ...

... selected for execution ...

As I continued through Park's dense passages, occasionally slipping into a rhythm that carried me along but mostly having to scrape and claw my way forward, I kept wondering what McFarland had meant by his grandiose descriptor. What was it within these tangled sentences, equations, and logic games that elevated *A Guide to Universal Grasping* beyond its peers, that toyed with, violated, and rewired the expectations of the genre? How did it create some sudden and pivotal break with the past? Was this in fact genius, or was McFarland a buffoon?

And what did it mean that I was ill-equipped to tell the difference?

It was then that I had the briefest moment of insight: as a tool for universal grasping, I was as poorly designed as the varied proto-bots Park decried for clumsily bumping their way through the aisles and shelves of his heavenly warehouse. Just as their appendages could adapt to only a narrow range of desired objects and failed over and over again to engage with materials they had not been preprogrammed to process, it was painfully evident that within the vast library where I worked, it was actually only a narrow band of books I could understand and appreciate. Or comprehend. Perhaps I remained a few steps ahead of those proto-bots, but surely someone, somewhere, was working on a replacement edition of me, a more intellectually agile version?

But we are problem-solving machines. As I circled back to the very beginning of Park's guide and read through it quickly again by focusing only on the phrases I'd underlined, I realized what I had in fact been doing: stripping away the complex technical details and extracting from this manual something else that was recognizable to me, something I knew how to interpret and catalog: a series of suggestive phrases that read like metaphors for human existence in an increasingly mechanized world. And not just interpret and catalog, but enjoy: as I reread those phrases, I knew I was bastardizing Park's work, but I was also creating from it something that spoke to, and even occasionally answered, my own hunger to master a kind of universal grasping that would allow me to be no stranger, nor a servile, programmed bot, in this warehouse of knowledge. A utopian dream that there was nothing around me that I could not grasp and reassemble into the discard library I was now building.

THE INDIAN WRITER SANTOSH PADHI IMAGINED a library created by his narrative avatar, Shackcham Thakre, a Mumbai demolition man, who collects books — on Venetian hotels and Parisian museums, on self-improvement and strategies for competitive mindfulness, on the romances of princesses and the penetrating gaze of an incorruptible police captain — through his work breaking down abandoned offices, foreclosed homes, and failed businesses. Whatever he can scavenge, he reassembles in a wrought iron shack, which is left open to the shantytown's youths, nurturing, in time, a subculture of washerwomen and rickshaw drivers and doormen who debate among themselves the evolution of modernist painting and the management theories of Peter Drucker.

✣ ✣ ✣

The Hell of Insects
Michael Maroun

In the introduction to his unorthodox anthology *The Hell of Insects*, the Uruguayan entomologist Michael Maroun shares that over a span of a particularly gloomy winter, three otherwise respectable and admired colleagues each approached him with a similar confession: either alone in their labs or out gathering specimens in the field, they had been spoken to by bugs.

Within the field, there is a widespread, though seldom discussed, awareness of a delusional parasitosis sometimes referred to as Ekbom syndrome, which leads people to believe they are being attacked or even eaten alive by insects, which has led victims of the syndrome to devise drastic cures involving Epson salts, vinegar, unregulated medications, antipsychotics, and even bathtubs full of insecticide. Many entomologists at one time or another have been approached by the friend of a friend seeking relief from such an assault.

The confessions Maroun heard were somewhat different, for the victims — these respected scientists — did not believe they had been bitten or stung, they did not believe that as soon as the lights were off their beds and walls with swarmed with bugs, but instead and even worse, they believed they had been spoken to, and the voices "had spoken as a One-Day Damsel Fly or a Striped Blister Beetle would have spoken, could it." Each of the entomologists who approached Maroun had been left shaken by the experience, increasingly dubious of his own ability to continue his work as a rational actor.

While Maroun was surprised by their confessions, what he felt most was a sense of relief, for he had heard the voices too.

A fixation with categories is, according to Maroun, a common trait of scientists, and true to this tradition, Maroun is quick to classify his peers. Microbiologists can be recognized not just by their white coats but also by their paranoia; astronomers are often blinded by their own vanity; geneticists are consumed by guilt; paleontologists by nostalgia. In this taxonomy, the unifying spirit of entomologists, Maroun argues, is shame: they understand that what attracts them beyond reason and consumes not just their waking thoughts but also their Freudian dreams is something most others find repulsive. And this shame makes it difficult for uncomfortable truths to spread through the profession. Silence reigns.

Sensing that he had tapped into something significant, at the 43rd Annual Gathering of International Entomologists held in Santiago, Chile, Maroun distributed an anonymous survey that asked, buried beneath many more innocuous questions about professorial mentoring, lab room bullying, and the economic returns of graduate degrees, if any of his peers had been spoken to by their subjects and, if so, whether they would be willing to share their experience. It created quite a buzz.

The conference organizers were outraged by the inclusion of this thoroughly unscientific question, which had the capacity to make their entire field — already the ugly stepchild of biology — a laughingstock. Of course, it became the main subject of conversation in every hallway and atrium, in the dark, lonely corners of the hotel bar. Ultimately thirty-four entomologists reported they had heard insects speak, and, perhaps even more surprisingly, that these insects had some insightful things to say. *The Hell of Insects* captures nineteen of these most unusual voices.

The dramatic monologues that make up the core of the book mostly fall into one of two complementary camps: either a cynical indictment of the human world or a seductive lure into the insect nest. We hear a cockroach's vision of the fragile human race being "snapped from this Earth like a dandelion's head," while the cockroach itself, "with this hard shell that protects me from diseases, from poisons, from the encroaching sun," continues ever onward.

A fly dismisses our pinnacles of beauty — "flowers, youth, paint and moon" — as the by-products of the simplistic structures of our eyes; could we, she suggests, see the world through her bulging, fractioned orbs, perhaps we'd have a deeper appreciation of the squirrel split across the road, for the complexities of dung.

An adolescent bee rhapsodizes about the ecstasy of nestling "one's face in the fragrant folds of a soft flower head."

And the butterfly who describes his own haunted transformation from creeping larva to winged angel and challenges his scientist: "When will you dare to change? Not to grow wiser, purer or more just, Not to age. But to dig into your body and find something strange?"

For reasons of job security, there are no attributions to the individual pieces — a gap that has led some more conservative peers to suggest the book is nothing more than a farce by Maroun, who, it has been whispered in internet forums and anonymous chat rooms, was already unlikely ever to get tenure and in desperate need of a second career. The few who have spoken up online on his behalf are hard to trace back to any tangible resumé or position, suggesting they are simply additional fictions sprung by Maroun, another attempt to populate his particular neuroses with fellow travelers.

As these rumors spread, they were soon followed by another: that Maroun had paid, from a state research fund nonetheless, to have his book printed on an unusually pulpy paper, bound by thickly starched glue and stamped by a rare ink, each of which is rumored to attract the silverfish, a nocturnal insect of the Zygentoma order that has been known to devour entire libraries. Its threat is so persistent and destructive that librarians across centuries and around the world have developed novel means of defense, ranging from repellent cocktails of camphor, turpentine, and boracic acid to the cultivation of bat colonies, which, it is hoped, will feed themselves on these bibliophile pests. If these claims about the book's physical nature were true, any private collector or public institution that housed a copy would be risking an infestation.

If one closely examines Maroun's author photo, a moldy copy of John Francis Xavier O'Conor's *Facts about Bookworms* (1898) is placed prominently on a shelf just over Maroun's left shoulder, beside a frame of mounted beetles.

(WHAT'S UP WITH ALL THE MEN? Surely they don't care about libraries more than women do, but possibly they are more prone to grandiose thinking and a permanently unfulfilled need to imprint the world? From what I've come across, women seem less focused on what a library might be and more willing to praise it for what it is: "Libraries are sanctuaries from the world and command centers onto it," Rebecca Solnit; "A library is a rainbow in the clouds," Maya Angelou; "When I got my library card, that's when my life began," Rita Mae Brown; "A great library is freedom," Ursula K. Le Guin; "The library is an arena of possibility, opening both a window into the soul and a door onto the world," Rita Dove.)

✢ ✢ ✢

Leopold's Jungle
Mats Vandroogenbroeck (trans. Knud Gyldenstierne)

The premise of *Leopold's Jungle* is that late in his reign the demented Belgian King Leopold II comes to suspect that the Congo, which has become the embarrassing focus of journalistic exposé and missionary outrage, is neither an actual colony nor even his vast, private plantation, but simply a ruse that has been perpetrated upon Leopold himself by an elusive network of agents and sycophants who wish to humiliate him.

As this story unfolds, Leopold has ruled the Congo Free State from an administrative palace in Brussels for more than twenty years, and it has made him obscenely rich. He has sent, or believes he has sent, thousands of his countrymen to harvest its riches. But he himself has never once visited his gargantuan estate. Perhaps the closest he came was nearly a decade ago when his capital city hosted a World's Fair, and Leopold awed the crowds by reconstructing three Congolese villages stocked with native men, women, and children who beat wild drums and paddled about an artificial pond in their dugout canoe. It was a marvelous show, and Leopold remembers to this day how eager he'd been in its aftermath to tour the Congo's rubber plantations. To ford its rivers! To command its natives! But time after time he'd been dissuaded by one aide or another warning him of malaria, mosquitoes, uprisings, or some other improbable nonsense. In retrospect, it is obvious that they were hiding something from him. Now it is too late: already in death's shadow, Leopold accepts that he will never touch his prize. And without ever once having seen the Congo himself, having never once sunk his fingers into its rich soils, he has no way of being certain it is real.

And the simple truth is, it seems *unreal*.

The reports he receives are barely believable: trees weeping rubber sap, jungles so dense they blot out the scorching equatorial sun, strange illnesses causing lethargy and chills, which primarily strike whenever true labor is required of the natives. As he looks out over his palace's manicured lawn at dusk, he struggles to reconcile what he has been told about the Congo with what he can see with his own eyes: the world isn't like that. Alone and awake deep into what may be his last nights, he cannot dispel this creeping doubt that while he has issued orders and decrees to guide the colony's exploitation, his ministers and agents had been laughing behind his back at their foolish king for having fallen for their tricks.

Trying to put his mind at rest, he stirs from bed to read and reread the letters and financial records he's been sent, hoping to discover within them some undeniable proof of the Congo's actuality. He is unmoved by the staggering profits they claim since he's certain they've all been forged. He wonders instead who spent the time to stain and batter their pages, to perfume them with burnt sap, to create this detailed and nearly convincing illusion of colonial administration. He can't help but acknowledge that whoever is behind this charade has a touch for detail and a perverse imagination. They'd sent him ivory and rubber. They'd sent him haunting, totemic fetishes, studded with nails, with distended genitals and breasts. And there were those natives at his fair. (Unless, of course, they'd been imported from Haiti or Brazil to play the parts?) In his deepening paranoia, he remembers the nights he'd spent listening to the hired guns he'd sent in those earliest years to map the Congo's infernal depths, when the land was still unknown beyond its coastal ports. It fills him with rage to have fallen for their fantastic tales of a dark interior.

And then the rage subsides. For although Leopold hates having been a dupe, how can he not also feel incredible gratitude to the person, or persons, who have worked so hard to convince him of what he has always wanted to be true? That the king of tiny Belgium rules an empire that dwarfs Europe. You could stuff proud Prussia, haughty France, and constipated Britain all inside his Congo and they could go straight to hell.

What Leopold can't grasp, however, is *who* could have created such a convincing, elaborate deception. He thinks of his cousin, the English Queen Victoria, but she'd never shown him any affection. He thinks of his daughters. Where are they now? Banished. Incapable of creating anything more than embarrassment. He thinks of his mistress, dear, childish Caroline, but he knows he's only been able to conjure her into being with the money this illusion has somehow made real.

Through long chapters dense as the Congo rain forest itself, Vandroogenbroeck lures his reader into an uncomfortable, compromised sympathy with Leopold, a sympathy that makes sense only if the very real and immense suffering Leopold did in fact direct — the death of millions — can be dismissed as a gross exaggeration or recast as a trick played upon Leopold himself. Like a doomed explorer, the reader becomes increasingly lost within Leopold's twisted logic and denials, increasingly unable to return to the world as it is.

Coiled on his desk, there is a ten-foot-long grotesque whip

*made of the jagged edges of hippopotamus hide that had been
gifted to Leopold by a returning administrator. The kind of
device one might stumble upon in a dream but never expect to
meet in our waking hours. A gift? What was the man possibly
thinking? Quietly Leopold had him striped of his pension.
And of course, there are his own Belgian papers, which used
to write triumphantly of Leopold's magnificent expanse. Now
on a nearly weekly basis they report of decimated villages,
famines, or revolts. Why print such things? No decent people
would want to read these lies over their morning tea or evening
pint. Perhaps his Belgians are as vile as he'd feared. And then
there are those documents, wherever he left them, seized from
an overzealous missionary. A ghastly photograph of a wicker
basket spilling over with severed hands. Punishment, the notes
say, for those who refuse to work. Why is it, he wonders, that the
proof of the Congo's existence, if that is what these objects are,
must be so horrible? Why not images of locals being civilized
and taught the Lord's Prayer? Of prosperous farms peopled by
radiant, grateful natives?*

✧ ✧ ✧

While there are countless books devoted to the crimes of colonizers
and, more generally, the horrors unleashed by our most unrestrained
rulers at home or abroad, there is also a smaller body, perhaps a shelf
or two, of "tyrant literature," which is distinguished by its humanizing
attempt to enter into their dictatorial, often homicidal minds. (And

which is not to be confused with "Dic Lit," literary works by dictators themselves, from Mao's "Little Red Book" to Saddam Hussein's *Zabibah and the King*, a romance novel in which a beautiful peasant girl falls hopelessly in love with the king, from Mussolini's potboiler *The Cardinal's Mistress* to the metafictions of Kim Jong-il, a catalog that spans, and sometimes blurs, spiritual manifestos, poetry, romance and memoir.) The art of tyrant literature is to continually straddle a thin, cutting line between understanding and accusation. This tradition has its seeds in Shakespeare's *Coriolanus* and *Richard III* but flowered in our totalitarian twentieth century with Gabriel García Márquez's *The Autumn of the Patriarch*, Zhang Jing Zhang's *Red Swan, Red River,* and Constantin Popescu's *In the Eagle's Talon*. None of these books, nor *Leopold's Jungle*, issues a pardon. They are focused instead on internal rot and madness as the inevitable end of absolute power.

Vandroogenbroeck's Leopold may be losing his mind but not his craftiness, and in the final chapter he at last begins to "remember." Wasn't there, he reminds himself, a wink and a nod when he sent Stanley off to map the interior, to claim a new state out of some unknown void? The bastard had probably spent his year drunk in a Turkish brothel, no wonder he looked so haggard on his return. How did they fool everyone with that ridiculous book and the territorial claims?

Of course, Leopold ultimately reasons, there is only one person so clever and foresighted, so visionary to have created this "Congo." Leopold himself. How could he have forgotten that this was all *his* brilliant invention?

Vandroogenbroeck:

The first mapmakers, Leopold reassures himself, had been right — Africa was just a vast, empty space awaiting a pen. The second maps he forged himself, winding that fat river like a whip through mountains and jungle, swamp and cliff. A labyrinth with no respect for geometry. He added villages here and there with the silliest names — Basoko, Bikoro, Budjala — some gibberish he mouthed while enjoying one girl or another. Wasn't that a game he'd played? He added trading posts, and even, to keep the peace, garrisons and churches. It was all as simple as writing the words, issuing the orders. Ah, to be king! His words become the world.

Even the heads impaled on sticks adorning his outposts, the swollen-bellied kids hung from the trees — none of it was real. That was the beauty of it all, the genius! His genius. The so-called atrocities were nothing more than the righteous rhetoric of outraged missionaries and so-called journalists. More of his agents. Yes, he remembers at last, that had been his wiliest stroke. Because you can't keep heaven to yourself. His Belgians, always eager for the easiest way, would have deserted their towns and cities in droves if he'd allowed his Congo to become a lost Eden. Only by making his hideaway empire a hell of early deaths and cruelties, and only by allowing — by ordering — those stories to leak back into his world along with all the rubber and flesh and gold, could he keep it all to himself.

Laying himself down to sleep in his thick linen sheets, at peace again, Leopold chuckles to himself and wonders how he had ever dreamt up something so horrible. And why had everyone believed it? It really was too much.

THE BRITISH WRITER CLAIRE-LOUISE BENNETT IMAGINED a vast, grandiose library built to satisfy the vast, grandiose ego of its patron. But on inspection every page of every book was as blank as his soul. Actually, that's not quite correct. Although it appeared that every page of every book was as blank as his soul, he was promised that somewhere within this library there existed a single book that, within a single sentence, contained everything. If he could only find it, he would, at last, be fulfilled.

✢ ✢ ✢

The Lucky One
Hyacinthe Danse

Around the turn of the twentieth century, French newspapers began to experiment with what they called *faits divers:* brief, fragmentary, and highly sensational stories that captured a glimpse of modern life, often in its most ironic form and without the depth of more traditional reporting. A woman is found dead from an overdose of barbiturates on a hotel bed scattered with roses. A father discovers that the burglar he stabbed in the dark was his own drug-addled son. Rival Romeos exchange bullets in the street while their common Juliet skips town with Mercutio.

What more is there to say?

At their best, *faits divers* captured sudden alterations in the course of otherwise ordinary lives, redirections toward new, often unwanted destinies. While they were secondary to the leading headlines and editorials of the day, they nonetheless distilled in their own distinct style the disorienting texture of a newly urbanized world, where our grandparents or possibly theirs found themselves surrounded by a perpetually evolving cast of strangers whose lives could be either perfectly mundane or as-of-yet-unwritten classical tragedies. If village life was suited to long tales told round a winter fire that reinforced a community's most basic values through the episodic adventures of beloved and recognizable heroes, the city was lurid, quick, and anonymous. The fact that *faits divers* were left largely unexplained corresponded to the inexplicable nature of modern life.

Perhaps the most artful practitioner of the form was the anarchist art critic Félix Fénéon, whose highly condensed and linguistically clever contributions were collected and ultimately published as *Novels in Three Lines*. More than a century later, Fénéon's work would inspire Teju Cole's "News from Lagos" series, bringing the form into the Twitter age, alongside a similar, though more gleefully fictionalized, stream of tweets from *Small Worlds*.

"Odd news but deeper truths too," Cole called their collective work.

I was reminded of this tradition while reading Hyacinthe Danse's speculative (i.e., incomplete, factually dubious, critically questionable) biography of Georges Simenon, *The Lucky One*, which is structured around fifteen moments from his life, fifteen moments that could be *faits divers* themselves. Each of these moments anchors a chapter, which then opens up into a larger portrait of a man who was, in fact, not so much opaque as overwhelming. Simenon's life was cobbled together through an abundance of words, travels, views, and betrayals that collectively suggest there is always something beyond what we have yet grasped, when in fact each next reveal is fundamentally a restatement of what's come before.

The truth, he acknowledged late in life, is too simple for intellectuals.

As a boy reporter, Georges Simenon would have been deeply immersed in the culture of *faits divers* and it certainly shaped his capacity to distill events into crystalline fragments as well as his deep cynicism. He went to work at just fifteen, when his father's death saved him from another tortured year of school, with his first assignment as a reporter for a conservative newspaper in his hometown of Liège, Belgium, working the police beat.

Within a few years he would put aside journalism for more

lucrative work, but he remained throughout his long life a compulsive reader of multiple newspapers, which he found more consistently engaging than the great novels of his time. The papers' headlines and smudged columns would help inspire the plots, characters, and details that ultimately filled the more than five hundred books Simenon would publish across the arc of his career, books that would make him the best-selling author of the mid-twentieth century with sales that still comfortably exceed those amassed by J. K. Rowling and Stephen King, although he has been matched by Danielle Steel and eclipsed by Agatha Christie. Some claim only Lenin has been more widely translated.

✢ ✢ ✢

The second of these moments captured by Danse is from German-occupied Liège in 1915, where the kitchen of the Simenon household has become a war zone unto itself. To provide for her family during these hungry years, Georges' detested mother, Henrietta, has taken in three German officers as lodgers, and these boisterous, triumphant men now share the crowded space around the Simenon's table and drink the Simenon's weak coffee. "Share" isn't quite right. They've claimed this apartment as more German territory. They laugh and stomp their feet, make rude jokes, pinch the boy's frail arms. Pushed to a corner, the unassuming father smokes his pipe and refuses to understand German, a language he speaks perfectly well.

In this time of scarcity, everything is rationed down to the potato, the dash of milk. At breakfast, each member of the household is allowed just a single boiled egg, but in the confusion of strangers and languages, observant young Georges sees his father slip a second into the pocket of his worn tweed coat before leaving for work.

Another son, painfully thin and just beginning to sprout, aching with so many hungers, might feel betrayed by the father's gesture. It's clear he hasn't taken the egg to share with his son but rather to fortify himself. Or possibly just to deny anything more of his kitchen to the officer, the leader of the wolf pack, who has now settled into his chair, boot on the table, shamelessly flirting with the lady of the house. In either case, Georges' reaction is something else: an unexpected spark of joy as the veneer of morality cracks like eggshell. His beloved father, the one who forgives all of his adolescent mistakes and violations, is a thief! And suddenly, for young Georges, a hero.

Nearly twenty years later Georges will bring his most famous creation, Inspector Maigret, into the world. Over the course of eighty-seven novels, Maigret, a large and slow-paced man, imbued with an attentive eye and unbearable patience, a man of deep appetites and unnerving drinking habits, a man supported by a loving wife, will solve many crimes, but unlike his famous peers Sherlock Holmes, Hercule Poirot, Tintin, and Miss Marple, he rarely carries the day through his cleverness or vast powers of deduction. In fact, as an author Simenon seems largely indifferent to the *how* of crime, centering his investigations instead on the more elusive *why*.

In interviews Simenon will explain that most policemen grow up side by side with the gangsters they later pursue, and they often have more in common with the thieves, in language and beliefs, even in their vision of right and wrong, than with the so-called innocent they are meant to protect. When Maigret gets his man, there is little sense of triumph of good over evil, but instead an affirmation of his clarity of vision: I see you, who you are and what you have done. Now let's have a drink together before you are locked away or sent to the gallows. The law will be enforced but not always morality.

✢ ✢ ✢

At the height of the Roaring Twenties in Paris, a gaggle of ambitious young men at a well-placed table drink champagne as they press around the evening's star, Josephine Baker, the exotic beauty from St. Louis who has become the talk of the town, perhaps the world. But one of the men, drunk like the rest, maybe drunker, and jostled by the crowd and his own anxious nerves, accidently spills his drink into the lap of his friend Georges. Everyone else laughs with glee. Now the party has begun! As a startled and then annoyed Georges rises to clean himself in the commode, Josephine, who's been pressed against him this entire time, brightens her eyes and laughs. She grips the crotch of his pants in both hands and slowly wrings the champagne from his trousers, silencing the table.

They've been lovers for the better part of a year, and although he's never been so powerfully attracted to a woman, certainly not his wife, he is becoming concerned by how this obsession is taking him away from his work. He's built what reputation he has around his legendary discipline, waking early each morning and forcing himself to produce eighty typewritten pages daily, an exercise so exhausting he'll often end it doubled over and vomiting like a marathon runner.

To make his work easily accessible to his readers, office workers and those with dirt under their nails, he is frugal, constraining his writing vocabulary to about two thousand words. By contrast, *Ulysses*, published just a few years before in the same city, is said to contain over thirty thousand and seems intended to be beyond comprehension. He's grateful, or so he claims, to spare himself the pretense of Literature, an idea that both repels and consumes him. Like his vocabulary, a narrow band of themes, locales, and ideas obsessively repeat, both in this early work and throughout his long career: prostitutes, police stations, mortuaries, traffic accidents, suicides, the suburbs, poisoning, criminal courts, asylums, crappy offices. Death by guillotine, alcoholism, suicide. Paralysis.

Working like this, Simenon can, in just over a week, churn out a new book — westerns, romances, adventures, dramas — which he publishes under one of nearly twenty pseudonyms as none of it is worthy yet of his true name. (In those days, most of his closest acquaintances knew him as Georges Sim.) Since coming to Paris less than a decade before, he's published nearly one hundred fifty titles, the exact count is elusive, and in one year alone he produced forty-four. But under Baker's spell? A sad, limp dozen.

If he is to win the Nobel Prize by forty-five, as he's begun to plot and even publicly assert, he needs to get serious. It is time to end the affair.

✧ ✧ ✧

While the public adores his pulp fictions and the Maigret series,

Simenon begins to write something else as well, a cycle of books he refers to as his *romans durs,* his hard or serious novels, books that do in fact begin to change his reputation and attract the praise of literary giants like André Gide, Thornton Wilder, and Henry Miller, books that will, at their finest, be favorably compared to those of Albert Camus. While he will write scores of *romans durs,* spanning decades and continents, a recognizable pattern runs through at least a considerable subset of the whole: a family man, generally someone who has led a responsible although undistinguished life, perhaps an accountant or a pharmacist, someone whose days are full of routine and predictability, suddenly veers off course. Perhaps he locks himself in his room and refuses to see anyone. Perhaps he boards a train and disappears into another name. Perhaps he suddenly commits a violent crime. Perhaps after suffering a stroke, rather than allowing himself to be healed, a man wills himself further and further into silence and retreat to the great confusion of his nurses and doctors, friends, and wife.

Despite this repetition of words and themes, his characters are consistently fully realized individuals, each unmistakably himself. His subjects are men, mostly but not exclusively so, who until some critical moment in their life had lacked the will to assert themselves and simply reflected what their families had demanded they be: men at the beck and call of more powerful, more assertive men. In Simenon's world, there is a perpetual desire to break free from the confines of moderation, and yet that dash for independence rarely ends well.

A curious obsession for a man who seemed to do whatever he wanted.

On a trip to a southern island — it's now in the early years of the Second World War — Simenon sees a poor, adolescent girl, a recent orphan he's told, in a red dress. There is nothing particularly distinguishing about her. She doesn't say anything. Her expression is blank. She isn't a great beauty. She simply stands in a doorway of a collapsing home in a red dress. Simenon could easily forget her, but he begins to imagine someone else who could not.

A country doctor, perhaps, on vacation with his wife and children, someone who, unlike Simenon, has never allowed himself a violation. A man in midlife who continues to cater to his mother's unreasonable whims. His family is having a bad time, cheated by the locals, sunburnt and tired. The food is poor. The hotel is poor. The island is without charm. But there is a girl in a red dress that the doctor can't put out of his thoughts, even after, or especially after, they've returned to the mundane patterns of their lives in their boring little town. He can't sleep. Despite his family's pleas and outcries, the country doctor will insist they return to the island the following summer, where he will, of course, pursue temptation, circle around it, nudge others toward it, and still never find what he lacks.

Disclosure: he ends up dead, back to the sun, floating in the bay.

While many of his characters are weak and easily corrupted, while they make bad decisions and injure, even kill, others, they are inescapably human and recognizable. Often the power of his books is rooted in their capacity to make us experience the world through the eyes of deeply realized people who've drifted beyond the realm of social norms, who've gone farther, into darker places. In *Dirty Snow*, perhaps his best book, Frank Friedmaier, another Belgian living in a

German-occupied zone, but this time during the second war, is the son of a brothel keeper. He is a humiliated and amoral man, who first murders another during a petty burglary and then assaults the rare woman who dares to show him kindness and affection. But when he is finally arrested, it is for a crime, one of the few, he didn't actually commit.

Critics dispute whether the central tragedy of Georges Simenon's life is whether, having established himself as one of the most popular genre writers in the world, he was consumed by a desperate and unfulfilled need to also be taken seriously, or whether, after he established himself as one of the most popular genre writers in the world, the public — and the academy, the judges — could never accept that he was in fact also a writer of serious and consequential work. Still others find the use of the word "tragedy" in either case a bit overheated.

There are those, quite a few actually, who believe that if Simenon had limited himself to, say, writing just fifty books, perhaps he would have produced a catalog of truly significant, era-defining works rather than a half-dozen that are easily lost within the cascade of volumes, and he might rightly be recognized as one of the century's greatest writers.

A smaller subset, more of the Borgesian school of thought, contends instead that as a writer of limited range, probably the best thing he could do was take a handful of themes and the same two thousand-odd words and slap them over and over again into combinations of one hundred forty to two hundred pages. That a half-dozen turned out to be memorable works is actually an extraordinary achievement or good fortune, and if he'd just had the will to churn out five hundred more, the odds are a few more gems would have tumbled out.

✢ ✢ ✢

A middle-aged Belgian man sits before a slot machine at a casino in Reno, Nevada, that smells of cheap gin and stale cigarettes. He loves the rootlessness of America, the long highways and flat motels, the anonymity, the release of new beginnings.

Yesterday he divorced his wife of twenty-seven years, Tigy, a woman he married when they were both poor, ambitious, and eighteen, and with whom he conquered Paris and traversed the world. Earlier today he married his secretary, a young French-Canadian woman, Denyse, with a large scar across her belly, an imperfection that would normally repulse him, but in this case, she has become an all-consuming obsession. She doesn't even pretend to read his books and refuses to believe he is truly famous on the Continent. He never loved Tigy this way. There's nothing to be done about it now, but he suspects he'll eventually hate Denyse with an equal passion.

He pulls the crank and watches the set of three metallic cards flip through all their iterations — race car, unicorn, baseball bat, dancing girl, full moon, sultan, martini glass — before settling on three hearts. Coins come pouring out of the machine and a crowd has begun to gather. It is the third time he's won in the last half-hour.

The people around him are drunk and cheering, but he is certain he is using up all of his luck to win the most trivial of prizes.

Simenon's approach to sex in many ways mirrored his approach to writing. Late in life he will claim to have slept with ten thousand women, an assertion that may be the most famous of all his many, many words. It's been repeated often, though rarely with its final lines: "... but one does not necessarily find human contact merely by searching for it. One generally finds a void, don't you think?"

With a roll of her eyes, one wife, the one he's just married, will tell another reporter it was more like twelve hundred. True to form, Simenon will also share that he rarely has had sex for more than two minutes and prefers not to undress.

His longest affairs, spanning decades and essentially creating polygamous households, were with the maids of his first and second wife, a repetition that seems to suggest a bias toward proximity and convenience over romance.

✥ ✥ ✥

By the early 1960s, Simenon accepts that he will never win the Nobel Prize. Five other Francophone writers have already taken it in his day: Gide, Mauriac, Camus, Saint-John Perse, and Sartre. After a bout of resentful depression, he writes a long biographical essay about Balzac, to whom he's often been compared for their shared capacity to capture the full breadth of society with their sprawling catalogs. Among other insights, Simenon concludes that Balzac was haunted by a fear of his own mediocrity and unloved by his mother.

It is a bittersweet moment a few years later when a grand three-day celebration is organized in Amsterdam to pay tribute not to Simenon himself but to his most famous but perhaps least literary character, Inspector Maigret. Although he has continued to write the occasional Maigret novel, he does so for money and with a sense of annoyance. The event is attended by all of his publishers, forty or more representing all the major languages of the world, by all of the actors who've played Maigret in varied films. A television studio is set up. There are tributes, banquets, and dancing late into the night. His marriage to Denyse is falling apart.

At the end of the party, he'll fly home to Lausanne and quickly write what he'll proudly describe as his "cruelest" book, *Le Chat*, a vicious little story inspired by his mother's second marriage. In it, a widow and a widower marry but quickly descend into mutual hatred and distrust. To protect themselves from poisoning (a recurring Simenon theme), both keep their private food stock locked away in separate cupboards. The only joy in the story is between the husband and a local barmaid with whom he conducts an affair.

✢ ✢ ✢

And one more: A seventeen-year-old, Simenon's daughter Marie-Jo, a girl so fragile she's been described by one of her many therapists as like a snail removed from its shell, is alone in her room reading from her father's latest novel, *La Disparition d'Odile*. Told with just the barest of discretion, the thinnest of disguises, it is the story of her own nervous breakdown, which occurred just a few months in the past. He writes so quickly, and his publisher is so eager to churn each volume into product, that she has barely had time to process the events herself before they are presented back to her in book form.

When they were younger, all four Simenon children would watch him, from an upper room in their grand home, while he paced in the garden. If he was deep into a new manuscript, and Simenon was nearly always deep into a new manuscript, they could tell by the way he walked with his shoulders curled up toward his ears, by the gestures of his hands, that he was becoming, perhaps the next two weeks, someone else. During those metamorphoses, he'd change his diet and drinking habits as well, and sometimes slip into a regional accent and adopt new pet phrases. He looked at his own children as if they were strangers.

Now she is the only one of the four who bothers to read his books, and she finds them all, like everything her father does, engrossing. But this particular volume frightens her. Nervously, she twirls the golden band she wears on her second finger, a gift that she begged him for at eight, and that she's since had stretched four times and continues to treasure.

With a dull pencil, she underlines several passages, including those where he is mistaken and those where he seems to have understood, and revealed to his vast audience, something about his daughter that she never wanted known.

Her suicide notes are always addressed to him and frequently quote from his work.

✜ ✜ ✜

The book closes with this quote from Simenon himself: "I was born in the dark and in the rain, and I got away. The crimes I write about are the crimes I would have committed if I had not got away. I am one of the lucky ones. What is there to say about the lucky ones except that they got away?"

THE SCOTTISH ARTIST KATIE PATERSON IS NOT JUST IMAGINING but creating the Future Library. She has planted a forest of a thousand spruce trees just outside of Oslo, which will be harvested in 2114 and turned into paper, which will then be used to print an anthology of texts commissioned by the library every year between 2014 and 2113. Margaret Atwood, David Mitchell, and Ocean Vuong have already contributed pieces that will be held, unread and in trust, for the next century.

✢ ✢ ✢

Days of 1931
Vasilis Vasilakis

In the mid-1990s, Vasilis Vasilakis published a new translation of C. P. Cavafy's collected poems. Although admired by those who read it, it was mostly challenged by irrelevance: at least four English-language alternatives already existed, each with a loyal following and a claim on future readers. Perfectly competent, sometimes artful, Vasilakis' version did nothing to refresh our appreciation of this great modern Greek poet. Like most books of poetry, even the fine ones, it went effectively unnoticed, selling, perhaps, a couple hundred copies, mostly to friends and family.

Discouraged, yes, but true writers keep it coming. Vasilakis followed this translation a few years later with a novella, *Days of 1931*, a fictionalized account of a single night in the generally mundane life of Cavafy. Again, not exactly a first. The opaque Cavafy has appeared in the fiction of Lawrence Durrell and Claire Kilbane, in the essays of Marguerite Yourcenar, in the songs of Leonard Cohen and Donovan, in the musings of Orhan Pamuk, and in the poetry of Yannis Ritsos, Mark Doty, James Merrill, and others. Something in his self-effacing, haunted presence is easily absorbed and reconfigured by others' imaginations. But while Cavafy has tended to haunt the shadows of other writers' works, Vasilakis allowed Cavafy center stage, which is perhaps a risk in itself. If the goal was to secure a wider audience, a novella about a mild-mannered, clerk-by-day, self-described "poet-historian" and nostalgic homosexual in an Alexandria long past both their primes hardly sounds like a publicist's dream.

What created a bit of a stir, at least on a few poetry blogs, was Vasilakis' decision to center this day around the writing of a single poem, and rather than selecting a Cavafy classic — "Ithaca," "Waiting for the Barbarians," or "Two Young Men 23 to 24" — he elected to write his own for this purpose and pass it off as one of the master's, an act of inverted plagiarism that different readers could interpret as arrogant, misguided, or daring. What struck me was that Vasilakis had to write an entire, albeit short, book of prose to get a single one of his poems into print.

Those who know a bit about Cavafy's biography can accurately assume that not a great deal is going to happen. In that sense, the novella is largely true to Cavafy's poetry, where the main events typically happen offstage or even far in the past; the drama of the poems is how those events are absorbed and refracted over time, how the past, either the personal past or a civilization's, is able to remain a vivid, plastic thing echoing through our lives.

When it begins, a long day at the Egyptian Ministry of Public Works where he has spent his last thirty years working has ended, and Cavafy is preparing himself to head out into the city as he has and will almost every night. The little rituals — combing of the hair, the English knot of his tie, adjusting his signet ring — are the little pleasures of a simple life. That and patience. Stepping out into the evening, he pictures the café where they meet, the same clustered tables, his spot saved, the friends beginning to gather. How dull it must be before he arrives, he muses in a rare moment of arrogance. No one wanting to waste their best lines until the audience settles. Over the past two decades, several dozen of his poems have been privately printed in pamphlets and broadsides, and his community has come to treasure him as a vital presence.

"While he is a clerk and a bachelor, a man of modest means and looks," Vasilakis reminds us, "he is also a Poet and therefore, in our secular world, something of a Saint."

Walking slowly through the sinking light of his city, he rolls lines around in his head.

He has been thinking lately about Oedipus, that strangest of ancient heroes whose first great test was not a feat of strength but a battle of wits with the Sphinx, a victory that should have heralded clarity but instead began a reign of first metaphoric and then literal blindness. Is that the fate of clever youth? Or perhaps, more likely, a consolation for older men who have given up on answers and come to accept that life is woven out of mysteries? The street is a dull one, the buildings tired and in need of fresh paint. The present is almost never enough, and our own stories can be so vague and halfhearted. Cavafy's Alexandria sits on the edge of the Greek world, both physically and in time, but all that history continues to surface up through its inhabitants.

He mumbles these half-formed lines:

> *These are unfortunate days for Thebes.*
> *That strange beast — they call it*
> *the Sphinx — for whom killing is not enough*
> *but asks riddles as well...*

And then he tries again:

> *It's hardly a riddle, really, when the Sphinx asks,*

> *"Why does every youth I let pass imagine
> that he is correct, entitled to kingdoms?"*

And once more:

> *For a time, we thought everything would be alright.
> Another king appeared and chased the beast away.
> But then there were locusts, and that horrible business
> with the queen. They say he really didn't know...*

But none of that is quite right.

At the café, a dozen or so men — "mostly hanging on to middle age, some with dyed hair combed carefully across their crowns, shopkeepers by day, merchants, minor officials, but all Men of Letters, minor or occasional poets, heirs of ancient Greece and thus guardians of Civilization itself" — cluster around the two small tables pushed side by side, their tiled surfaces covered in espresso cups and cognac glasses, cigarettes and ashtrays, a folded Athenian paper, a fresh volume from France.

Nearly half of Vasilakis' novella, in many ways a love letter to a lost world in which friends would gather each Wednesday and Friday night to share the news of our great nothingness and to talk together about ideas that just might paper the void, is devoted to this scene, and he describes each of the men (they are all men) in fine detail, capturing both their individual voices and how individual voices knit together into conversation and exchange, mirroring evenings shared by friends over the centuries. They talk about their health and about books, about what they've heard from the broader world through the letters they receive from children and past lovers. Eventually the conversation turns to a recently published and not, they mostly agree, particularly successful essay written by one of their absent companions.

Cavafy himself weaves in and out of their talk while discreetly observing his fellow men; most of what is recorded could be his tracking of the night. Without losing the train of their conversation, he finds himself particularly intrigued by "the doctor," a regular among them who remains uncharacteristically remote this evening. While the others launch their witticisms, push their gossip, pose their questions, and charge forth with replies, his only response is an indifferent, tired smirk or a skeptically raised eyebrow. Eventually, with his second coffee nearly drained, the doctor studies their grains. As though emboldened by their cryptic message, he begins at last.

What he shares is the news, apparently unknown to these friends, that a former member of their circle, one Amaril, was found dead in faraway Naples.

For a moment the room is hushed, and then the disbelief, the memories. When they finally settle and ask for detail, the doctor continues: Amaril took his own life, it seems. There was a question of money. Apparently, his new business, the hotel they'd all heard so much about, that he'd financed with a loan from his father-in-law, was bankrupt. And there is also talk that that boy, the actor, had left him. For some time, their conversation circles through the past and the stories they'd sometimes shared and sometimes held only to themselves of Amaril.

Eventually they disperse into the dark night.

Walking home by the most indirect of routes, Cavafy strolls by the taverns, the cafés, the alleys. He issues half greetings to half strangers. He passes the shuttered shops, the lit windows, and offers discreet glances to the young workers who are absorbed in other pursuits. He has always been drawn to this time of night when nothing is fully itself and it is easiest to blur the past and present, the fluid and the fixed, lowly sailors and the greatest of heroes. As the darkness settles, it takes the faces longer to pass through the smoke they blow, for mouths and their words to weave together. He watches them from the corner of his eye, so that the faces form like a puzzle, feature by feature. For an instant, each one is only an unpossessed curve of jaw, a teasing smile. Fragments of some whole that can never quite be reassembled but are all the more suggestive for their incompleteness.

He hears music and singing somewhere a little off in the night, but it is moving away from him.

It was on one of these streets that he first met Amaril so many years ago, when they were both young men so full of secrets and shame. Walking past a shop that sold cheap and shoddy merchandise to day laborers, Cavafy glanced through the window — dusty though it was, and half obscured by the glare of light — and saw him, in profile. Against all his better reasoning, Cavafy made himself enter the shop and pretended to take an interest in some gaudily colored handkerchiefs, and soon this assistant was there beside him, displaying the wares. Although there was so little to say, they managed to talk for a while about the colors, the texture of the cloth, some other nonsense, their hands close to one another. At the back of the room, the shopkeeper sat oblivious, lost in his smoke. Or maybe not, Cavafy realizes now; maybe he was deeply amused by this unconvincing charade?

For a month they were together, often in borrowed rooms or those that could be rented cheaply for a night. Were his eyes blue? Sapphire. They must have grown dull and ugly with time. But not tonight: it's still that month for as long as Cavafy can keep summoning it back, with all its trembling and fatigued delight, the things half seen that have lingered through the decades. The perfumed hair. When Amaril abandoned him, it was for an invitation to stay at a villa along the sea through the most stifling of summer months as the guest of wealthy man.

When they finally did see each other again, some years had passed. While Cavafy stayed rooted in Alexandria, Amaril had been to Beirut, to Chania. Somewhere along his path Amaril had deserted their disreputable ways for another destiny, surely one arranged by his parents, or at least grown far more careful. When each little kingdom was offered to him — a business, a wife, a reputation, a lover — he took it without any fear of what lurked inside. As though they were truly his and not just gifts on loan from the gods of irony. As though everything had been promised to him. As though he'd solved the one riddle and no others would follow. He greeted Cavafy warmly but with a blankness in his eyes that obscured any past.

Back at his desk, Cavafy opens the window wide, inviting in both sea and city. Although it is late now, he takes up his pen and begins to write.

IN THEBES

There is so much talk of the scandal now,
its violent end. Oedipus, it seems, really didn't know
that he'd married his mother. With his own hands,
he gouged out his eyes. And yet (while the others gossip on),
I still see him before all that, coming down
from the pass: smiling despite the Sphinx's blood,
his bright eyes daring us not to call him king. His swagger —
how it unsettled the queen — as though he really did believe
there is only one riddle and he'd answered it.
Not one of us had the nerve to tell him he was wrong.
Not one had that desire.

THE AMERICAN ARTIST ED PARK IMAGINED the Invisible Library, a collection of books that have never actually been written but are referenced in other works of art — titles like Hernando Garcia Leon's *The New Age and the Iberian Ladder* (from Roberto Bolaño's *The Savage Detectives*), Eli Cash's *Old Custer* (from Wes Anderson's *The Royal Tenenbaums*), Oolon Colluphid's *Where God Went Wrong* (from Douglas Adam's *The Hitchhiker's Guide to the Galaxy*), Geoffrey Bannon's *The Sand Book* (from Colin Hamilton's *The Thirteenth Month*), and Vivian Darkbloom's *My Cue* (from Vladimir Nabokov's *Lolita*). Such a library could not actually be built, of course, but in its place, Park is assembling an ever-expanding online catalog of its nonexistent contents.

✢ ✢ ✢

A Museum of Winter

In design, *A Museum of Winter* reminds me of the DK series I knew well from my own household: *A History of Medieval England, A Guide to Space, An Introduction to Dinosaurs*. Each published in large format with vibrant pages adorned by carefully cropped photographs against a stark black or white background and scattered with blocks of informative text. Books designed to break down facts and histories into discrete component parts, little nuggets of knowledge that can then be consumed by young, hungry minds. Few illustrations, no first-person voice. Unlike the DKs, however, *A Museum of Winter* forgoes any list of author, project editor, art editor, designer, researcher, et cetera, as though what is being shared transcends any individual and reflects instead the collective knowledge of a community, a culture.

And what, then, does it convey? *A Museum of Winter* examines this peculiar season through its phases and rituals, and so there are pages, or open two-page spreads, on, for example, "The First Snow," which includes sub-passages on the exhilaration children feel anticipating the possibility of canceled school, the hunt for last year's boots that may or may not still fit one's growing feet, the agitation of pet dogs pressing their noses against our windowpanes. Other sections include:

> *The varieties of snow and their implications for snowballs*
> *and snowmen.*
> *Games played on ice.*

Colin Hamilton

The Nutcracker and other seasonal performances.
Fall babies.
Stories best told around fires.
Gradations of cold, frozen toes, and fingertips.
Frozen things that can be touched by the tongue and things that cannot.
Cultural traditions associated with polar plunges and the science of their medicinal claims.
Darkness, sleep, and depression.
Sudden blizzards that rerouted history.
Objects both lost and discovered in glaciers.
The geometry of snowflakes.
The kindness of neighbors.
Sounds associated with frozen, brittle objects.
Silence.
Boredom.
The longing for spring and the first sight of returning birds.
The madness of April storms.

Had *A Museum of Winter* been written for an equatorial audience, for youth who'd never seen the sun set in midafternoon or felt icy water leak through their boots and into their thick woolen socks on a long walk to school, it's easy to imagine its exotic appeal, just as I was mesmerized in my childhood by accounts of Pacific islands and Arabian deserts. But clearly its publisher had something else in mind, so that the reader is offered a glimpse not around the curvature of the Earth but back through the spiral of time. As a "museum," its elegiac ambition is to capture, to freeze, a lost world, or at least one that is rapidly being lost — a lone Siberian tiger pacing rhythmically, neurotically, in a cage. Written not so much for our children but for theirs, who may never know this defining season except through legend.

In that sense, *A Museum of Winter* is best classified as a ghost story, and not the kind our children clamor to hear over and over again, snuggling closer to us and seeking some playful excuse to sleep at the foot of our beds or between their parents, not the kind that ends with a mask being pulled off a monster's head to reveal a familiar face, but rather the kind that stays alone on the shelf, always present, ever informative, gratefully unopened.

THE ENGLISH ARTIST MATT HAIG IMAGINED a Midnight Library that exists in a liminal space between life and death. Should you find yourself there, linger. Within its walls, vast but not endless, are books describing the various lives you might have led. On any given shelf or aisle, the books may seem rather repetitive, for not every choice is of grave consequence, but as you wander further into the far and poorly lit sections, you will be increasing startled — sometimes relieved, sometimes at a loss — by what you might find.

✧ ✧ ✧

The Great Balzoni Disappears
Aron Schmitz, abridged and illustrated by Simon Stein

Like every other boy on his block, Benjamin Weisz was raised to think of petty theft as a sport, but not yet having mastered misdirection — the common thread of crime, magic, and art — he sometimes ended up in the policeman's grasp. At thirteen, however, he discovered two things more gratifying than picking pockets: the ecstasy of escape and his talent for it.

For a time, he became increasingly reckless, even hoping, it seemed, to get caught. To steal a few coins might fill his belly for an hour, but to break free from cuffs or the back of a paddy wagon? To divine the internal logic of a lock? That filled his soul. That awakened some secret sense of self that had been obscured by the generalities of childhood and hand-me-down clothes. It soon became evident that no chain or cell could hold him. One day this gift would make him world famous, but first it made him a neighborhood hero, the most daring of the boys.

An entrepronourial friend added this insight: why steal from people if they would be willing to pay to be conned? Soon their townie gang was staging events in the back rooms of pubs and by the broken fountain in their neighborhood park. They would allow strangers to manacle Weisz's hands behind his back and sometimes his ankles too before placing their bets. They'd tug tightly at the chains, assuring themselves of their reality. Weisz began to intuit these wagers were not so much about *his* ability to slip free as they were about *the audience's* own sense of entrapment and despair, their own thwarted dreams of release. When he escaped, it became just possible, just for a moment, that we might all someday be set free.

While the boys enjoyed this game, it wasn't long before no one in the neighborhood was willing to bet against Weisz. So, they took their show down to the docks at the far side of the financial district, where they draped Benjamin in heavy, looping chains. Sometimes they'd blindfold and sometimes gag him as well before tossing the adolescent boy into the bay's murky water for the entertainment of bankers and the office girls they'd taken out for drinks. He would sink twelve feet down and rest amid the oyster shells and rubbish. After a tantalizing, tortuous minute or two that often felt longer, the surface water would resettle, only to be tickled now and then by a quick ripple of bubbles. At last, when the cheers quieted and the nervous laughter became an anxious silence, Weisz would break through, gasping for air and igniting applause. Coins filled the upturned hat. We are told:

> *Weisz's escapes came naturally, almost effortlessly. But there was an art he still needed to master: performance. There were some days when he'd free himself too quickly, almost, it seemed, with the mere shake of his wrists, and as a result the audience barely had time to register his achievement. And so they were denied the satisfaction of their own hearts racing, of realizing that they themselves has been, unconsciously, holding their breath as well and were about to burst. On those occasions, rather than joy or relief, those who'd come to watch were left with a sense of having been cheated. Which they didn't care for at all. These men, these rich men, paid for danger. To watch someone else stumble on the edge of death. The wallets opened widest when Weisz could convince them that the possibility of*

failure was very real or even, better yet, inevitable — if not this day, then the next the locks would deny his tricks and pin him to the bottom of the sea. That kept them coming back for more.

Before long, Weisz learned to speak about dying at every show. "I suspect the Grim Fiend is following me," he said, in a resonant and mysterious voice that was quickly replacing his own, as he'd dry himself carelessly on the dock, allowing the worn towel to slide from his bare young chest. "He may catch me someday yet."

From Weisz's original awakening, other private, more brilliant escapes followed: from his eight city blocks, from these first friends, from his family and their Jewish name, from his accent, his own poor taste, from consequence. Each time he released himself from one of the world's little locks, he felt a mad, liberating joy, like the roar of a crowd when he arose gasping from the frothy sea, the chains sinking beneath him.

A decade passed.

✢ ✢ ✢

Decades pass for all of us, at least the lucky ones. I must have still been in college when I first read *The Great Balzoni Disappears*. It was a time when cloaking myself in a certain nihilistic darkness reassured me that I was, despite all evidence to the contrary, a serious person, which, at the time, seemed like an admirable thing to be.

Like so many of the books I've read, it left very little with me that is tangible. Certainly not any of its particular words, no signature phrase. Even the plot is hazy to me. A rise and a fall, that much I remember. Also the cover: a kind of kitschy psychedelia that gave *The Great Balzoni Disappears* the patina of genre fiction.

But I do remember the character of Weisz, the escape artist who can't stop escaping, the illusionist who comes to doubt the reality of the world around him. Those ideas spoke to me at a time when I myself was changing so dramatically, when I was both filled with a desire to become someone new and unnerved by how easy it was to do so — as though there was no core to my being, and thus no shape I couldn't reconfigure myself into. After all, most adolescents either are or are aspiring to be escape artists.

I hadn't thought about the book for many years, but then I caught a notice in a catalog that it had been "rediscovered" and was being reissued as a graphic novel of all things. It made sense, in a way. There was always something a touch cartoonish about the story, all that vaudeville, the twirling, Edwardian mustaches. More than anything else, I took it as a sign of our times that for an older book to find new audiences, it had to be abridged and illustrated. Apparently, that is what Simon Stein does, convert other people's novels, especially those in need of rediscovery, into graphic formats — *Ice, The Plains, I Served the King of England, The Memoirs of an Anti-Semite*. What an odd destiny to not write your own books but to retell, and yes, streamline, those of others? To mine them for a few gems. There must have been a time when Stein imagined his future quite differently.

Most things, if they survive at all, do so by becoming smaller, fragments of a former whole — the six anthologized poems out of a collected thousand, the shard of a once whole Grecian urn. I was mildly intrigued when I first read about this graphic *Balzoni*. And then distracted. And then I forgot all about it. One of my colleagues must have been more attentive and ordered a copy for our library, which explains why, a few years later, this new incarnation of it found me as I was shifting through a cart of recent arrivals in the discard room.

I couldn't resist.

Or I saw no reason to resist.

Or I had nothing better to do, other than my job, so I found a place to sit and began to read.

✢ ✢ ✢

A decade passed.

Weisz, or the Great Balzoni as he has renamed himself, is now performing in cities across Europe, and especially in those countries where the police are called "secret" and his escapes, which are complemented by a routine of magic, illusion, and sleight of hand, are cheered as Everyman's escape from the State's stern locks. He has left his original companions far behind and travels now with a small entourage: four Portuguese porters who transport his props, the straitjackets, mirrors, rabbits, and trunks; a Prussian manager who negotiates with the theaters and press; and his current assistant, the lovely and adept Magdalena, whom they found swinging on a trapeze in a circus in central Bohemìa just as their previous girl was growing tiresome.

Everything is going well. Every performance is sold out, and wherever they travel Balzoni is a prized guest at the grandest of parties.

It's champagne and oysters. Their flyers pass hand-to-hand on the streets and in cabarets but also in offices and government buildings.

Then one day in Budapest, a distraught but vaguely hopeful Magdalena announces she is pregnant.

As he absorbs her words, Balzoni realizes he will have to leave her, in the next town or the one after that. He's rather fond of her and sorry to do it. She's good on stage as well, but the road is no place for a child. And he? An illusionist, not a father. With a little luck, which he's never been short of, he suspects he can find some family, an innkeeper or former stagehand, maybe a widower or one with a bachelor son, who can be paid to take her in. It shouldn't take too long to find a new girl whose parents will be relieved to be rid of and train her in. Until then, however, the show must go on.

They continue to perform every afternoon and night, but her timing is off on their well-rehearsed routines. What are meant to be enticing, distracting gestures are clumsier than before. That won't do. Magdalena should be prettily invisible, but her awkwardness is catching the audience's attention — not just at those critical moments when she is meant to divert their gaze, but when it should be returned to him. It's all part of the same carelessness that landed them in this spot. He's preparing to set her straight or even cut her loose, but in the dressing room that night she collapses. A doctor is called and when he arrives, the men are quickly ushered out. Some time passes as do first coffees and then a few worried schnapps before the doctor emerges with the news: she's lost the child.

Although Balzoni's knows he should feel relief, it is as though all the air has been punched out of him. What kind of man, he asks to his own surprise, would ever even have considered abandoning her in this state? There is a sudden gaping horror at this own being, at his emptiness. Grief and shame knot themselves around him, the tightest locks he's known. When he visits her the next afternoon in her hotel room, carrying an armful of flowers that are soon scattered across the floor, they weep together for the first time — she for their lost child, he at his own selfishness.

But weeping, he can't help but notice, is a strange thing.

It's almost as though it's not just tears that have poured out him, but also along with the tear all these dark emotions — grief, shame, suffering, loss, doubt — that had been shackled to him, that had twisted him into a monstrous state, that had pulled him back into her arms, begin to slide off him one by one. When he realizes that he is no longer in their grasp — that they were, in the end, just another kind of escapable chain — and that he has emerged once again unbound, he is startled by his own virtuosity and the freedom it entails. He could almost laugh at the madness of it. That despair thought it could imprison him! His impulse is to take a little bow, to make a rousing if over practiced speech about rising above those things that seek to ruin us.

For an accomplished illusionist, every room is a stage.

But not every person is an audience.

If he has escaped from despair and its manacles, Magdalena has not. Easing back into a chair, he observes how she remains snared in her pain. Like a cage, it binds her knees to her chest, her head to her hands. It seems to choke the very breath from her. For a moment, at least, he concedes their roles have somehow been reversed, and now she is the one commanding, even earning, the audience's gaze. This should annoy him, but he's never been afraid to learn from other performers, and he realizes there is something compelling in this act of hers. It is almost like a strange Russian ballet. He recognizes a tinge of pity or at least concern running through him, but what he primarily feels is that most precious of responses — rapt attention. To see her embrace this pain rather than struggle against it, as though she were afraid of losing it too. It's quite a show. And as tempted as he is to help her break free of it all, he is also curious to understand how this despair of hers works.

When she finally speaks, it startles him. Not just her words but the physical presence of her voice that has somehow escaped from the hell she's in, that has crossed out of it like a lasso and tried to pull him back in. More ropes that seek to wrap about him. Hot, infernal ones. Magdalena: "I should have known you couldn't bring anything into this world. Whatever part of you was in that child, it could only disappear. Everything you've ever touched slips through your hands."

As Stein brings us deeper into Balzoni's story, his illustrations take on greater responsibility for representing not just the physical world but also the characters' experience and interpretation of it. The early pages and panels are crowded with words, but they slowly thin out as the tale progresses. Magdalena's accusation is, in fact, the final written passage of this abridgment. What follows is achieved entirely through graphic effect. I believe it is an accurate accounting.

Balzoni's first impulse is to scoff. What he understands better than anyone else is that to escape from something is the opposite of losing it. To escape is to understand a trap's intricacies so well that you master it; that it becomes yours. Nothing slips through his nimble hands. Nothing evades his immense attention. In fact, it is only his heightened presence in this world that has allowed to him navigate it so deftly. How else could a simple pickpocket like himself have become a hero not just adored by the masses but dined by industrialists, applauded by statesmen? Only a fool, and there is no shortage of them, would allow himself to be bound to reality. What he understood before the rest of them is that everything is a choice: duty or freedom, the past or the future, pain or nourishment, grief or indifference. The secret to all of his escapes is simply to turn the lock that others fail to see, to change.

But something about this moment has him stuck in place.

He's aware that he can't take his eyes off Magdalena. He can see how her hatred, of him, keeps fighting through, overpowering her grief. That she isn't trying to escape her misery at all, but rather to burrow deeper into this darkness. To cradle it.

Balzoni closes his eyes. He begins to imagine himself in his trick tank filled with water. His face is pressed against the glass panel and a crowd is beyond it, watching the last bubbles trickle from his nose. Or so they believe. Although he could free himself at any moment, this is the point in the act when he must choose between two paths. Some days he'll give his audience fear, his eyes bursting as though he's suddenly realized that this time — this one, last time — something has gone horribly, fatally wrong. Other days, he'll stare back at the crowd defiantly, as though he may very well drown but he'll never be defeated. He has never known which of the two expressions is the more mesmerizing.

Watching Magdalena now, feeling how her hot, tear-stained breath sours the room (an effect Stein achieves by a progressive yellowing of the panels), he suspects it hardly matters. It could be fear or defiance; it could even be his mad, private joy. It is always that human moment when, it appears, the performance has cracked, that allows the audience in. Any of those recognizable emotions becomes something his audience can grasp onto, a means of binding themselves to him. Isn't that what their tickets buy them? The right to own him for an evening, to experience the world through him?

For the first time, he thinks that perhaps he's the one who has been tricked. That each time he imagined himself having broken free, all he'd actually done was exchange one cage for the next. In the end, what's the difference between sealed in a tank upon a stage and being carried triumphantly through the streets, supported by a dozen arms, their hands tight around his ankles, thighs, and wrists? A cage of bars, a tank of glass, a net of flesh.

Maybe he's never escaped anything at all. And in that moment, he can envision the thinnest, most resilient of cords, which he'd somehow never seen, winding back through the years and tying him to the boy he'd once been.

And at that moment he begins to envision a different performance.

The real threat is not the chains but these people, these people who always demand something more from him. Who seem to think that when he escapes from a burning ring, from a dangling rope, he is somehow *returning to them*. What a fool he's been, raising his arms in victory like a conductor inciting his orchestra to roar, allowing their applause to envelop him. Tomorrow they'll get a surprise, and he must start practicing it now.

The ice tank is the climax of his current show. As he thrashes within it, churning the water, even those in the farthest corners of the theater, in the cheapest seats, feel their lungs ache in chorus with his. Not again. At his next show, he'll hardly struggle at all, just work the locks diligently, and when he does emerge from the tank, he will project not triumph but resignation. Almost disappointment that Death has rejected him once again and left him here, abandoned to the audience's claims of praise and possession. Wouldn't that be the ultimate escape? The one true escape? To reject their ecstatic celebration, to deny them the right to join him? To free himself not just from his chains but also from those who want to knot themselves to him? To give them nothing. Nothing at all.

When he imagines their stunned silence, he feels himself smirk. Finally, when he turns his back on them, someone will boo. A first, soon followed by others. The theater will echo with their anger. When he leaves the stage something permanent will have been broken between him and the audience. He'll walk out alone, at last.

Or, perhaps, he'll go still a step further. He'll embrace the metal chains, let himself sink into the waters and rest there at the bottom, not even pretending to escape but staring back at them. Then, at the final moment, as the final mystery, the great mystery, is about to be revealed, he'll close his bright blue eyes that have, until then, been locked on those of a young woman in the front row. And he'll keep it all to himself.

As he looks up from his thoughts, you can see in his eyes that he expects to meet Magdalena's and to find in her attentive, approving gaze all he needs to know, but she is still staring at her own hands, her fingers knotted in some twisted puzzle all their own, holding on to something he can't quite see, that he'll never touch.

THE ITALIAN WRITER GIORGIO VAN STRATEN IMAGINED a collection of lost books, ones that were in fact written, or that van Straten believes were written, but that no longer exist, having been destroyed by self-censorship, disruption, war, and, most commonly, fire before they could achieve the security of wide publication. Van Straten's library includes Lord Byron's *Memoirs*, which were burnt in his publisher's fireplace presumably to save multiple reputations when simple greed would have dictated its preservation, and Nikolai Gogol's sequel to *Dead Souls*, which was meant to be the *Purgatory* to its *Inferno*, and which the author himself burnt just ten days before his death in despair at his own literary imperfection coupled with deepening religious fanaticism, as well as a thousand-plus pages of Malcolm Lowry's *In Ballast to the White Sea*, which was meant to be the *Paradise* to *Under the Volcano's Inferno*, that went up in flames along with the rustic cabin, free of plumbing and electricity, where Lowry was living in British Columbia.

✣ ✣ ✣

A History of Book Burning
Lynn Pearson

Perhaps *A History of Book Burning* caught my eye among the refuse of the discard room because I had recently reread an old story by the future director of Argentina's National Public Library about Qin Shi Huang, who, after bringing an end to a period known as the Warring Time by conquering all his foes and reuniting China under his rule, famously and perhaps apocryphally ordered both the construction of the Great Wall *and* the erasure of written history within its confines. Protected from savages and the past, he was then free to initiate another grand project: directing all the empire's sages and alchemists to concoct an elixir of life so that he could reign forever. It is likely that his early demise is linked to the consumption of their mercury-laced experiments. He was buried, by his own decree, within a city-sized mausoleum that flowed with poisoned rivers, eternally guarded by a six-thousand-member terracotta army.

Or maybe it was simply its glowing, glossy red and black cover, the bold yellow lettering, that set it apart even in a poorly lit corner of the discard room?

From the brief author bio at the back, I read that Pearson was a fellow librarian in a city that has long held a hazy fascination for me after I spent a single night there half a lifetime ago and thought I might have fallen in love with my best friend's cousin; it was a time in life when falling in love was rather easy, in fact, problematically so.

The reasons we pick up one book versus another are varied and bend to their own logic.

And the reasons we write them, too.

In Pearson's case, she was in her first year at the library, fresh out of graduate school, when to her surprise she was invited — via word of mouth, there were no written details — by a colleague she hoped to befriend, to a book-burning party. When she expressed alarm, she was laughed off. It was a tradition, she was told, and fun, an annual event they hosted every August 22nd. Don't bring *Fahrenheit 451*, she was told, we've already done that! She was also warned not to mention the party to anyone else because, for obvious reasons, the administration disapproved.

In this cloak of silence, Pearson had no way of knowing who else among the staff had been invited and whether this was a widespread event or a gathering of a select few, but over the days that followed she felt there was a different hum about the lounge, whispers in the aisles, winks across the arcade, a nervous anticipation of coordinated violence. She herself had been uncertain of what to do, both appalled by the theme of the party and, to her embarrassment, grateful, as a new employee, as a shy young woman living alone in a strange town, to have been welcomed into some kind of secret.

When the evening eventually rolled around, she found her way to an unkept backyard not far from the university campus where maybe thirty or forty of her peers had gathered, an odd assortment of the library's prized collection of eccentrics. The attendees had all been instructed to bring something to drink, that was essential, and something to burn. There was just a little coolness in the evening air, and the surviving mosquitoes had all grown fat, sluggish, and increasingly bold in their final attempts to pierce the soft flesh at the back of human necks like lonely undergrads at the tail end of a dance.

It was an awkward night at first, which might just be to say it was a gathering of librarians outside of a library, but as evening finally gave way to dark and someone began feeding logs — not so much firewood, really, but broken limbs and refuse gathered throughout the summer — into the fire, it began to rage in a way that stirred something unexpected within Pearson.

As the flames rose higher, popping red embers up into the sky and down onto the dry grasses, the host, a low-ranking librarian who often ran afoul of both the administration and the union and who, in punishment, was continually moved from one branch or department to the next, began to speak by welcoming his guests and reminding them of the rules. Then he called them forward one by one, and the librarians took their turns standing before others and making the case for why the book they'd brought should be burned.

There were plenty of easy targets: the latest vampire erotica; a vapid biography of a horrible monster who'd been the hero of a previous generation; some dated novel that stood out even among its unenlightened peers for its misogyny and racism; ten simple steps to corporate and then world domination. Someone brought Ayn Rand's *Atlas Shrugged*. Someone else stepped forward holding up Cormac McCarthy's *The Road*, which was followed by Rumaan Alam's *Leave the World Behind* and Steven Pinker's *Enlightenment Now*.

With each proposal, there was a shocked gasp from the crowd followed by a practiced but not always well delivered speech of accusation from the librarian, which was met with a combination of cheers and jeers. Then, at the very last moment, as the book dangled above the fire and the accuser's wrists would begin to glow and twitch in the heat, as if by an elegant, intuitive choreography, someone else would step forward to defend the offending volume.

Yes, its politics were odious and childish, more white supremacy wrapped up in the gray hood of libertarianism, but reactive resistance only emboldens these views.

Yes, it was essentially a zombie book that kept its readers gripped by threatening to murder and eat a child while preening about in a cloak of literature, but haven't once beautiful writers earned the right to become parodies of themselves?

Yes, some books read as though they've been written as rough drafts of made-for-TV movies but isn't it important to leave future generations a concise record of our cliches. Not the outliers of thought but the most common denominators?

And isn't the clearest view of the world from the shiniest, highest tower?

Soon the festivities were getting into the swing of things and the offers were bolder and more transgressive. Pearson remembers seeing, flickering above the flames: *The Catcher in the Rye, Harry Potter and the Sorcerer's Stone, Maus, The Absolutely True Diary of a Part-Time Indian, Lolita, The Adventures of Huckleberry Finn, Beloved, Go Tell It on The Mountain, Crash, Two Boys Kissing, The Satanic Verses.* The more indignant the accusers became, the more they wound their language into something that resembled logic but wasn't, and the harder it became to discern if anyone actually meant what they said or the precise opposite.

Slowly at first and then quickly, what began as a series of practiced speeches became a mob of people, of *librarians*, shouting back and forth across the flames. *Burn it! Are you mad? Burn it! Never!* They were on the cusp of amassing themselves into a rally, but that really wasn't their way and soon the party broke back down into its composite parts, fragmenting into side arguments and laughter and realignment. Some drank even more ambitiously then, while others slipped off, two by two, into the shadows.

Although the fire was dying down, Pearson could sense a flame of sorts still flickering among them. They'd exposed something to themselves, dared themselves to do something destructive, but given the choice they'd collectively embraced their better angels and reaffirmed who they were, who they were going to go be — the Defenders of the Book, Champions of Free Speech and Intellectual Curiosity. They'd tested themselves, and they passed. They were good. Like the best of rituals, the night had brought all of its participants closer, and by saving every last book, they believed they were saving themselves.

They next day they were back at their posts at the information desks and checkouts, a little bleary-eyed and befouled but proud, helping good citizens navigate their collections. And no one suspected they'd ever considered another way.

Pearson wasn't so sure.

The ritual had *changed* Pearson, leaving her uneasy, uncertain of who she was and what she might be capable of, because in the thrill of the night she'd felt the temptation of the flames, which in her case was not so much about burning any particular book as it was the desire to destroy something precious, to violate, to extinguish.

Being a librarian, she sought to understand herself through

reading, and so she began to research the surprisingly long and varied history of book burning, which led her all throughout the library, for she learned there was no section that hadn't been reshaped by this story, that didn't bear its scars. As the accounts of book burning piled up around her, becoming overwhelming in their exhausting, alarming repetitions across cultures and eras, she began to develop a taxonomy to make some sense of it all.

✢ ✢ ✢

Pearson defines five basic categories, three of which she refers to as "the classics" and two as "primarily modern variations."

The first are those conquerors who burned the books of the vanquished in acts akin to scattering salt on once-fertile fields or desecrating the bodies of the dead, where victory is not sufficient but the enemy needs to be humiliated, hollowed of its past, stripped of its future.

As far back at 330 BCE, Alexander followed his victory over Darius by marching into the Persian capital of Persepolis and burning its archives to the ground. In 1193, or possibly 1197, a marauding Muslim army stormed through far northeastern India. Cities and fortresses fell before them, treasure was amassed, but these insatiable violators were drawn relentlessly toward the Nalanda monastery, which for more than six hundred years had been a center of Buddhist practice, built around a library that contained an unparalleled collection of both Buddhist and Hindu texts. When the Muslims put the vast collection to the torch, Nalanda is said to have burned for six long months, and when flames finally died out, so did the practice of Buddhism in India for centuries to follow. Following the Reconquista in Spain a little more than three centuries later, the fanatical cleric Cardinal Jiménez de Cisneros organized the burning of as many as two million Muslim books, which was followed by a ban on writing in Arabic and the ownership of Arabic books, a language and tradition that had preserved classical Greek learning throughout the Middle Ages.

Sometimes the destruction is more instantaneous: on a single day, July 12, 1562, a single person, Diego de Landa, the bishop of Yucatán, burned virtually every last Mayan codex, a collection of hundreds or even several thousand. Now only three remain, and Mayan philosophy, religion, and astronomy have been reduced to mostly incoherent fragments of once-complex thought.

This category of book burning excelled in our middle centuries as long-distinct civilizations came into sudden, violent contact with one another, but the practice continued into the modern era: in the War of 1812, vengeful British troops burned the fledgling U.S. Library of Congress, and seventy years later they burned the Burmese royal library. Libraries were targeted in both World War I and World War II, including the Belgian library at the Catholic University of Louvain that was torched by German troops in 1914, destroying not just the spirit of Belgian resisters but also many irreplaceable Renaissance and Gothic works and one of the only written examples of a rare Easter Island language. UNESCO has estimated that a third of all the books in Germany were destroyed during World War II. During the ethnic cleansing of the Yugoslav collapse, the Serbs used incendiary grenades to set fire to the National and University Library of Bosnia and Herzegovina in what is believed to be the largest act of book burning in modern history. As recently as a few years ago, sexually repressed fundamentalists motoring across Mali targeted Timbuktu, which has been a center of learning and book culture for centuries, burning libraries that contained rare medieval documents in Arabic, Songhai, Tamasheq, Bambara, Hebrew, and Turkish. In this otherwise ugly story, a handful of brave librarians managed to smuggle several hundred thousand manuscripts to safety.

✧ ✧ ✧

There are those who burn other people's books as an act of cultural warfare, and then there is Pearson's second category: those who burn their own history, including political writing perceived as seditious. Of these, the most notorious, the most grandiose, is the second-century BCE Chinese emperor Qin Shi Huang, mentioned above, who undertook a vast program of book — and scholar — burning so that history could begin again with his reign.

At about the same time, a Consul of Rome ordered the "burning of all books of pretended prophecies," which in effect amounted to books that might question the inevitability of things as they were, which might legitimize some alternate future. As Rome passed from republic to empire, more books were sacrificed. A little over a century before the Spanish destroyed the Mayan codices, the fourth *tlatoani* Itzcoatl (these are the Aztecs) ordered the burning of all historical records as though they were rival siblings that might claim his throne.

✧ ✧ ✧

The third category is related to the second but distinct. Rather than seeking to eradicate alternative histories and futures, these book burners selectively targeted books they categorized as heretical, a practice that dates back, at least, to the fifth century BCE when Protagoras' *On the Gods* was burned in the Athenian agora for its impiety and atheism. Over the millennia this has been, principally, a religious specialty played out as Jews, Christians, Muslims, Hindus, Buddhists, and others have fought among themselves to codify beliefs and orthodoxy. There are hundreds of examples, maybe more, but two flagged by Pearson were slightly different and caught my imagination: in the 1520s or 1530s, the alchemist, physician, and freethinker Paracelsus publicly burned books by the Greek Galen and the Persian Avicenna because they were still taught in universities despite containing serious medical errors, and in 1842, the director of the school for the blind in Paris ordered the burning of all books written in braille.

As Pearson notes, burning books and burning the people who read them, or wrote them, were often intertwined.

✧ ✧ ✧

For all three categories, book burning had symbolic power. It wasn't just books but an enemy's spirit or soul the violator sought to destroy. But they should not be confused with symbolic acts. Real books were burned and, in many cases, driven out of existence. In some, only a few, rare specimens survived if they were properly hidden and suppressed, often for generations, sometimes centuries. The most accomplished of book burners largely predate Gutenberg and the advent of mass publication.

Once books became widespread, once it was almost always certain another copy existed somewhere, what it meant to burn them also shifted in meaning. Thus, Pearson's fourth category, what she calls "performative book burners," with roots in Savonarola's Florentine bonfire of the vanities, but which Pearson considers a primarily modern practice. The intent of performative burners is rarely to actually eradicate the offending books but rather to incite outrage and even to forge some new, terrifying sense of identity through the vilification of books and those who read or write them. In the 1870s and 1880s, U.S. Postal Inspector Anthony Comstock, a "weeder in God's Garden," and his New York Society for the Suppression of Vices burned more than fifteen tons of books while successfully lobbying Congress to enact the Comstock Laws, which made it a crime to use the post office to transfer obscenity, contraceptives, or even personal letters with sexual content. Books, Comstock claimed, "are feeders for brothels," and his men wore a badge divided in two: on one side, a purveyor of vice is being locked away; on the other, an upstanding citizen (recognizable by the top hat) is piling books into a fire. Performative or not, the damages are deep and real: Comstock bragged of driving fifteen people, include several leading suffragettes, to suicide.

And then, of course, there are the jackbooted Nazis who staged highly public burnings of "un-German" books by Jewish authors and other "degenerates" to lure their ready followers across yet another line so that, as Goebbels said, "the German folk soul can express itself again." As Heinrich Heine predicted, "Where books are burned in the end people will burn."

During the Pinochet dictatorship in Chile, books of leftist literature were burned as were books on cubism, which were thought to be about the Cuban Revolution.

Imitators and admirers still rally today, as every librarian and schoolteacher knows.

Most but not all performative book burning is ideological: in *The Library Book*, Susan Orlean describes a possible act of arson that set the Los Angeles Public Library aflame in 1986 and damaged more than one million books yet went virtually unreported nationally, because across the world Chernobyl was melting and closer to home the stock market was tumbling down and down. Or, because the populace had grown indifferent to the image of a smoldering library. One of the most visceral details from a book cobbled together from myriad details: even decades later, many of the books that survived the fire and remain in the collection still smell of smoke when opened.

✢ ✢ ✢

Pearson's last category is the most distinct: those who burn would-be books in their manuscript form before they can come into existence. Here too there is a long history, of both those who succeeded and those who, at the last minute, wavered. It begins, in Pearson's telling anyway, with Virgil, who at his death asked his unwilling friends to burn the unfinished and imperfect *Aeneid*, but Pearson primarily focuses on more modern examples driven by shame, fear, and sometimes meanness.

After Emily Dickinson died, her sister burned all of her letters and considered burning her poems — if that's what those were — as well. After Sylvia Plath committed suicide, her husband, the poet Ted Hughes, burned the last of her journals, which is thought to have contained details of their marriage and Hughes' infidelity. At William Blake's death, friends burned many of his unpublished works that they considered to be too scandalous, too freethinking, or simply lacking in quality. A prison guard confiscated and burned a novel an unknown Jean Genet had written while he was incarcerated, because Genet had written it on stolen sheets of rough brown paper that were meant instead to be stitched into bags, and because Genet was a vile pain in the ass. The original Irish publisher of *Dubliners* panicked at the last minute, fearing he'd been lured into not literature but pornography, and burned all but one copy, which Joyce managed to obtain "by ruse," and which he used to re-create the book when another, bolder publisher finally took it on five years later. Kafka, who all his life was haunted by a sense of shame and worthlessness, famously asked his friend Max Brod to burn all his unread papers — including unpublished manuscripts for *The Trial*, *The Castle*, and *Amerika* — at his death, a request Brod rejected out of hand.

Not only did Brod protect these papers, but he strove to make Kafka's unconventional, disturbing work more accessible by omitting unfinished chapters, adding titles to some stories and aphorisms, and shepherding fragments into what could be read as coherent wholes.

Still closer in spirit, THE SPANISH WRITER CARLOS RUIZ ZAFÓN IMAGINED a hidden library he called the "Cemetery of Lost Books," an asylum for books that have lost, or simply never found, their readers. It is bound by mystical rules rather than the pragmatic ones of space management or supply and demand: only special readers are allowed in; they can take just a single book; they must keep it forever.

✢ ✢ ✢

About the Author

Colin Hamilton has helped create a library, a center for dance, affordable housing projects for artists, and a park. He is the author of a poetry chapbook and a novel, *The Thirteenth Month*. A graduate of the Iowa Writers' Workshop, he lives in St. Paul.

About the Type and Paper

Designed by Malou Verlomme of the Monotype Studio, Macklin is an elegant, high-contrast typeface. It has been designed purposely for more emotional appeal.

The concept for Macklin began with research on historical material from Britain and Europe dating to the beginning of the 19th century, specifically the work of Vincent Figgins. Verlomme pays respect to Figgins's work with Macklin, but pushes the family to a more contemporary place.

This book is printed on natural Rolland Enviro Book stock. The paper is 100 percent post-consumer sustainable fiber content and is FSC-certified.

The Discarded was designed by Eleanor Safe and Joseph Floresca.

Unbound Edition Press champions honest, original voices.
Committed to the power of writers who explore and illuminate
the contemporary human condition, we publish collections of poetry,
short fiction, and essays. Our publisher and editorial team aim
to identify, develop, and defend authors who create thoughtfully
challenging work which may not find a home with mainstream
publishers. We are guided by a mission to respect and elevate
emerging, under-appreciated, and marginalized authors, with
a strong commitment to advancing LGBTQ+ and BIPOC voices.
We are honored to make meaningful contributions to the literary
arts by publishing their work.

unboundedition.com